Goddess Girls

APHRODITE
THE
FAIR

Goddess Girls

APHRODITE
THE
FAIR

JOAN HOLUB & SUZANNE WILLIAMS

Aladdin

NEW YORK   LONDON   TORONTO   SYDNEY   NEW DELHI

This book is a work of fiction. Any references to historical events, real people, or real places are used fictitiously. Other names, characters, places, and events are products of the author's imagination, and any resemblance to actual events or places or persons, living or dead, is entirely coincidental.

ALADDIN

An imprint of Simon & Schuster Children's Publishing Division

1230 Avenue of the Americas, New York, New York 10020

First Aladdin paperback edition December 2014

Text copyright © 2014 by Joan Holub and Suzanne Williams

Cover illustration copyright © 2014 by Glen Hanson

Also available in an Aladdin hardcover edition.

All rights reserved, including the right of reproduction in whole or in part in any form.

ALADDIN is a trademark of Simon & Schuster, Inc., and related logo

is a registered trademark of Simon & Schuster, Inc.

For information about special discounts for bulk purchases, please contact Simon & Schuster

Special Sales at 1-866-506-1949 or business@simonandschuster.com.

The Simon & Schuster Speakers Bureau can bring authors to your live event. For more

information or to book an event contact the Simon & Schuster Speakers Bureau

at 1-866-248-3049 or visit our website at www.simonspeakers.com.

Book design by Karin Paprocki

The text of this book was set in Baskerville Handcut.

Manufactured in the United States of America 0918 OFF

4 6 8 10 9 7 5

Library of Congress Control Number 2014949905

ISBN 978-1-4424-8827-4 (hc)

ISBN 978-1-4424-8826-7 (pbk)

ISBN 978-1-4424-8828-1 (eBook)

We appreciate our mega-fantastic fans!
Lana W., Lida L., Sandra L., Michelle W., Raven G.,
Valentina M., Lulu M., Camila M., Nadira B., Justine Y.,
Melanie C., Jennifer R., Stephanie V., Adara R., Katie M.,
Stephany I., Emma J., Dream Y., Ally M., Caitlin R.,
Hannah R., Dana P., Madison W., Sara S., Paris O.,
Amy S., Ashley C., Prisca M. & Izabel K., Sophia O.,
Juliana N., Camille C., B-B., Meghan B., Zoya B., Katya B.,
Charlotte D., Brooke G., Helen X., Olivia H., Angelina D.,
Diana G., Sarah M., Emily M. & Daniel M., Emma W.,
Sydney G. & Hailey G., Jasmine R., Ella S., Lea S., Kayla S.,
Ariel S., The Andrade Family, Alba C., Abby G., McKay O. &
Reese O., Angel H., Elizabeth R. & Olivia R., Caitlin R. &
Hannah R., Lilly T., Christine D-H. & Khanya S.,
Linda H., Jamison C.G., Micci S., Kaylee S., Kristen S. &
Erin K., Jessie F., Lily-Ann S., Alexandra E.S., Jamie E.S.,
Lindsey A., Eden O., Andrea C., Evilynn R. & Ruthie B.,
Sydney B., Mia A., Megan D., Camila M., Valentina M.,
Luciana M., Cece F., Kendall H., Lilly H., Lillia L., Ashley D.,
Shannon Y. And Tiffany Y., Grecia V. & Yasmin V.,
Virginia J. & Shelby J., Sophia R., Tiffany W., Reilly H. &
Ashley H., Annie K., Divine N., McKay O. & Reese O.,
Alyssa D., Tawney K., Jenny C., Grace H., Tamera W.,
Sidney G., Karis C., Shelly B., Sue F., Amanda W., Michela P.,
Britney D., Danielle H., Victoria B., Caitlynn L., Vickie H.,
Rachel B., Diane G., Samantha S., Jenn H., Sofia W.,
Izabel K. & Prisca M., Heather H., Michelle J., Lorelai M.,
Emeline K., Mariana P., Whitney Z., Ariel C., Sadie T., Keira
J., Vivian Z., Marielena B., and you!

–J.H. and S.W.

CONTENTS

1

Happy Birthday, Ares!

Aphrodite

S HH!" **APHRODITE WARNED THE CROWD OF STU-**
dents gathered in the open-air domed cupola at the top
of Mount Olympus Academy. "He's coming!"

Instantly, the students hushed, all shooting looks
of excited anticipation at the cupola door. Aphrodite
straightened her chiton. It was cotton-candy pink with a
scalloped hem and an off-the-shoulder collar—the latest

style, worn especially for this occasion. Fluffing her long golden hair, which she'd threaded with sparkly pink ribbons that matched the color of her chiton, she took a quick glance around the room.

She noted with satisfaction the cute shield- and helmet-shaped balloons that floated above the students. Gold and silver streamers had been wound around the tall columns that encircled the inside of the dome. Then the columns had been hung with crisscrossed toy swords and spears. These were all decorations that the guest of honor would appreciate once he arrived.

The knob on the cupola door turned. At the very last second, Aphrodite struck a dramatic pose, one hand on her hip. "Surprise!" she yelled when the door opened to admit the muscular, blond-haired godboy of war. It was Ares, her crush.

Everyone joined her in the shout-out. That was quickly followed by calls of, "Happy birthday!"

Another godboy, Apollo, who had brought the birthday boy here pretending it was for band practice, now ushered him inside.

Ares's blue eyes widened in delight as he took in the scene before him. "Whoa! This *is* a surprise!" Catching Aphrodite's eye, he smiled. "Did you do all this? I can't believe you managed to keep it a secret from me!" he added when she nodded.

"It wasn't easy," Aphrodite admitted, smiling up at him. Then she shot a sideways glance at a winged girl with short, spiky orange hair who stood nearby.

The girl's iridescent orange-feathered wings ruffled. "Hey! I can keep a secret when I have to!" she protested. As she spoke, words puffed from her lips in small, white little cloud letters to hover over her head where anyone could read them. She was Pheme, the goddessgirl of gossip and rumor.

Several students looked up to read her words and then laughed. Most times, telling Pheme anything was like broadcasting it to the whole world. Especially now that she wrote a gossip column for *Teen Scrollazine*. However, Aphrodite was sure that Ares's look of total surprise had been real. Which meant Pheme *had* managed to keep the news of this surprise party a secret. From *him*, anyway. No doubt the girl had told everyone else about it!

"You did really well," Aphrodite reassured the girl.

"Yeah, good work," added an apple-cheeked boy with shimmery golden wings. It was Eros, the godboy of love, who was Pheme's crush. Pheme grinned back at them both, obviously pleased.

Aphrodite was about to tell Ares more about how she and her friends had managed to sneak around making all the birthday preparations, but just then Apollo clapped a hand on his back. "Happy thirteen, god-dude," he told Ares.

"Yeah, congrats on officially becoming a teenager like the rest of us," a turquoise-skinned boy added in a teasing tone. It was Poseidon, god of the sea.

As more of Ares's godboy friends swarmed around to congratulate him, Aphrodite's three GGBFFs, Athena, Persephone, and Artemis, came up to her. GGBFF—as in Goddessgirl Best Friends Forever! It was a nickname Athena had come up with recently. It had just slipped out when she'd gotten superexcited about going with her friends to a new fun park that included a snorting beast called a Minotaur at the center of an amazing maze.

"Anything we can do to help?" Persephone asked. In her arms she was cradling Adonis, the black-and-white kitten she and Aphrodite shared the care of.

"Thanks for the offer," said Aphrodite, giving the kitten a gentle rub under its chin. "There's not much to do until it's time for cake, though."

As Adonis stretched and began purring, Persephone reached a hand up to adjust the yellow-and-white daisy she'd tucked behind one ear in her curly red hair. The flower had begun to droop a bit, but at her touch it instantly sprang to life, fresh as if newly picked. She was the goddessgirl of spring and growing things and had the greenest thumb of anyone at MOA.

"Besides, you guys have already helped out so much," Aphrodite went on. "I never could've gotten everything ready in time without you." That was an understatement. Plans for the surprise party had been in the works for the last two weeks. Her three friends had written out invitations, set up chairs and tables, put up decorations, *and* helped with snacks.

"Happy to help," said Athena. The blue-gray-eyed goddessgirl was the brainiest of Aphrodite's besties. Athena's dad was Zeus, the principal of the Academy.

Persephone nodded. "Yeah, it was fun!"

"And that's what friends are for," agreed Artemis. Her glossy black hair was caught up in a cute, simple twist high at the back of her head and encircled by golden bands. Usually a quiver of arrows and an archery bow were slung over her shoulders, but she must have left those in her room for once.

Noticing that her three dogs were sniffing around the big round birthday cake at one end of the snacks table, she called to them. "Amby! Suez! Nectar! Get over here, guys. Cake is for guests. You'll get snacks later." Wagging their tails, her bloodhound, beagle, and greyhound obediently trotted off to investigate the gifts table instead.

Athena leaned over to Aphrodite. "Hey! Ares's cake looks fantastic. Good job!"

"Thanks," said Aphrodite. She was rather proud of the two-layer cake she had baked and frosted it herself. It was chocolate with blue icing, Ares's favorite kind. And she'd stuck blue and green candles on top. Thirteen of them, of course. "I actually wanted to make it in the shape of a helmet, but that proved too hard for my limited baking skills," she admitted with a grin. Just then, a burst of laughter from the group of godboys standing around Ares drew the girls' attention.

"Remember the first time I met you?" Apollo was saying to Ares as the other godboys listened in.

"It was first grade," said Ares, nodding. He looked happy, which made Aphrodite happy. She'd really wanted him to enjoy his party!

"Yeah," Apollo went on. "When I asked who you were,

8

you practically bit my head off. 'I'm the god of war!' you shouted. 'So you better not pick a fight with me, 'cause I'll win!'"

Poseidon chuckled. "Yeah, coolheaded Ares is not."

The other boys laughed knowingly, and Aphrodite couldn't help smiling. Ares had a reputation as something of a bully, largely deserved. Still, his hot temper had cooled a lot in the past year. Everyone said she had a calming effect on him, so she liked to think she could take a little credit for the positive change.

A big grin spread across Ares's face. "Yeah, I remember," he said to Apollo. "You said, 'Okay, then, I won't fight you.' And we just threw some javelins around instead."

"And the rest, as they say, is history!" Apollo gave him a friendly mock-punch on his shoulder and Ares just laughed.

As other boys jumped in to tell more stories about

Ares, Aphrodite gazed fondly at him. In her humble opinion, he was handsomest godboy at the whole academy. And though there'd been some rocky moments between them in the past, they'd had smooth sailing for quite a while now. Which boosted her reputation as the goddess of love. Good thing, too. Because mortals and immortals alike might not trust her to help them with their love problems if she couldn't help herself!

Just then, Ares slipped away from his godboy friends and came over to give her a hug. "Thanks for all this. You are so awesome!"

"Well, I had a lot of help," she told him. Feeling pleased at how well everything was going, she gestured toward Athena, Persephone, and Artemis. Her friends had moved over to the snacks table to munch on chips, though Artemis seemed to be feeding her dogs more than she was actually eating herself.

"So . . . cake first?" Aphrodite nodded toward the snacks table and then glanced toward a second table behind it that was laden with gifts wrapped in colorful pieces of papyrus. "Or would you rather open your presents?"

"Presents!" Ares exclaimed, rubbing his hands in excited anticipation. The students close enough to hear him laughed.

Minutes later, he was seated before the gifts table, his blue eyes gleaming. While the other students watched, he pulled his first gift from the stack—the one Aphrodite had gotten him, as luck would have it.

She held her breath a little. Would he like what she'd brought him? Without even looking at the tag that identified who it was from, he quickly ripped off its red-and-pink heart-patterned wrapping. She was pleased to see his face light up as he opened the box.

"Awesome!" he exclaimed as he pulled out a brand-new pair of supercool winged sandals. They were the mega-popular "Fly like the Wind" kind from Mighty Fighty, a store beloved by MOA boys. In addition to various athletic sandals (all embossed with the store's *MF* logo), the shop carried equipment including bows and arrows, spears, javelins, and shields.

"Thanks, Aphrodite!" Ares called out.

"Guess he didn't need to read the tag to guess who that gift was from," Persephone teased Aphrodite, which made everyone laugh.

"Yeah, the red-and-pink-heart goddess-of-love-looking paper was pretty much a dead giveaway," Artemis added, chuckling.

Aphrodite grinned at her friends, then called back to Ares, "You're welcome!" She was so glad she'd picked just the right gift.

Ares tore through the rest of the gifts in no time at all, exclaiming over each new one with genuine delight. Most of the boys had gotten him athletic or battle equipment from Mighty Fighty or scrollbooks about war.

Some of the girls had gotten him little papyrus bags of nuts and dried fruits, or baskets of fresh peaches, pears, and pomegranates. Athena had gotten him Homer's just-published second book, *The Odyssey*, which was about one of the greatest heroes of the Trojan War.

There were gag gifts, too. Like spears that squirted bright-colored washable paint, bobble-headed toy monsters, hair gel to restyle "helmet hair" after an especially long and hard fight, and a tunic printed with: KISS ME, I'M IMMORTAL!

When the last of the gifts had been opened, Ares looked around. "Is it cake time?"

"Sure! I didn't bake it just to sit here and look

beautiful." Aphrodite laughed and waved everyone over to the snacks table.

Once the students had gathered around, Apollo's band, Heavens Above, struck up the Happy Birthday song. Although Ares was a band member, he sat this one out. Literally. He was now sitting before the table in a chair Aphrodite had decorated with streamers. There were balloons tied to the back of it that had BIRTHDAY BOY printed on them. Athena helped her light the cake's thirteen candles, while Persephone and Artemis stood nearby, waiting to help with serving.

Curious about what was going on, Adonis suddenly leaped from Persephone's arms into Ares's lap and tried to sniff the cake. Aphrodite gasped. But before she could stop the kitten, Ares settled an arm around it.

"Whoa, furball," Ares said, cradling the kitten in the curve of one muscled arm. "This is *my* birthday cake!"

He smiled up at Aphrodite. "But maybe you can have a teeny bite . . . with some *mice* cream." Which cracked everyone up. Still cradling the kitten, Ares took a deep breath and then inched forward in his seat a little.

Aw, thought Aphrodite. She sighed happily at the sight of the big, strong guy cuddling the kitten. They looked so cute! She wished she'd thought of having an artist attend the party to draw pictures of scenes like this. *Wished?* Hey, that reminded her . . .

"Wait!" she exclaimed before he could blow out the candles. "Don't forget to make a wish first."

"Oh, right," said Ares. His brow furrowed in thought a moment. Then he drew in another big breath, puffed up his cheeks, and blew out all thirteen candles at once.

"Good job!" Apollo leaned over to high-five him. In a teasing voice, he said, "I always knew you were full of hot air but that—"

BAM! The door to the cupola flew open so hard that it smashed against the wall!

Apollo broke off the rest of what he'd been going to say as all eyes swung to the doorway. Since Hera had stopped Aphrodite in the hall only that morning to say that she and Zeus would try to drop by during the party to wish Ares a happy birthday, Aphrodite half-expected to see them standing there. Zeus was not only MOA's principal, he was also King of the Gods and Ruler of the Heavens. A powerful guy, he often tore his own office door from its hinges. Not because he was angry, necessarily, but because he didn't know his own strength.

However, it wasn't Zeus and Hera who stood framed in the doorway. It was a petite, energetic-looking girl wearing a purple chiton. Her straggly, purple-streaked black hair was tied back in a ponytail, and her skin shimmered slightly, the mark of a goddessgirl.

She looked about eleven or so, but she definitely wasn't an MOA student or anyone Aphrodite knew. And she had not been invited to this party; that was for sure.

The party-crashing girl set the school bag she was carrying on the floor beside the door. *Thonk!* Sounded like there was something heavy inside it. Then she placed her hands on her hips and glanced around the room, like she was searching the crowd for someone. When her deep blue—almost purple—eyes found Ares, a calculating gleam came into them. Her lips curled upward. With a slight edge in her voice, she said, "Happy birthday, little brother. Bet you didn't think I'd make it!"

Huh? Aphrodite's head jerked backward in shock. Ares has a *sister*?

2

Eris

Ares

ARES CRINGED, STARING IN HORROR AT THE girl who'd just crashed his party. *Oh no. My sister!* Having her turn up here in the cupola had most definitely *not* been his wish when he'd blown out the candles on his cake just now. Far from it. He'd wished to win the Temple Games, a series of athletic war game competitions, which were to take place at the end of next month.

He and some of the other guys were going to start training for the games tomorrow.

"E-Eris?" he sputtered in surprise as she headed straight for him. Although she was short and so petite that she looked younger than him, she was actually older. He glanced over to see Aphrodite staring between Eris and him in confusion. Panic filled him. He had to get rid of his sister before she ruined everything for him here at MOA. How had she managed to find out about his party, anyway?

In the almost seven years Ares had been at MOA, he'd never told anyone about her. Including Aphrodite. And with good reason! Eris had made his life such a misery before he'd come to the Academy that he'd tried to forget she existed once he got here. And mostly he'd been able to do exactly that, except for brief visits home, during which he always tried to stay out of her way.

Eris's glance flicked to the kitten in Ares's lap as he continued to stare at her, aghast. "What's the matter? Cat got your tongue, brother?" she asked, giggling. That laugh of hers always had a slightly mischievous, possibly even *evil*, sound to it. Why had she come? he wondered.

Apollo and Poseidon stepped forward to block her way when she moved farther into the room, heading straight for Ares.

"Hey, it's okay. He really *is* my brother," Eris told them. When Ares didn't deny it, the boys moved aside and she marched up to where he sat.

"Cute kitten," she told him. She stretched out a hand to pet Adonis.

Ssss! The kitten, who was usually friendly toward everyone, ducked his head to avoid her hand. And hissed. And leaped from Ares's lap, scratching his leg in the process.

"Ow!" Ares yelled. The kitten scampered over to Persephone, jumping into her arms to eye Eris suspiciously.

That cat was a good judge of character, thought Ares. If he could've run from his sister right now without looking like a coward, he would have, too! Instead, he just studied her warily and mumbled, "Hi, sis."

She grinned at him. "Long time no see." Then she jerked her head toward his guests. "Aren't you going to introduce me to your friends?"

"Hey, everyone. This is my sister, Eris," Ares said in a less-than-enthusiastic tone.

"Hi," chorused the students, but their faces were full of questions. Especially Aphrodite's. Still, now that the ice had been broken, they began to swarm around his cake.

Ares stood and moved to stand protectively by Aphrodite, slipping her hand into his. She elbowed him gently, sending him a look that plainly said, *Duh, hello? You have a sister?*

Then she flashed a smile at Eris. "Nice to meet you." Loosening her hand from his clasp, she began pulling the candles out of his cake. "Welcome to MOA. I'm Aphrodite. I can't believe Ares never told me about you."

"Really? *Never?*" Eris wagged a finger at Ares and said playfully, "And *you* never told me about *her*. But I read a certain gossip column in *Teen Scrollazine.*" She glanced in Pheme's direction. "So I already knew you two hang out."

Ares didn't read Pheme's column in the scrollazine. But he figured it was probably full of gossipy tidbits about all the immortals on Mount Olympus. He sensed a potential threat behind his sister's playful tone. Had she come here hoping to wreck things between him and his crush? It's the kind of thing she *would* do. Her idea of fun.

Aphrodite picked up a knife and began to cut the cake. Her three best friends busied themselves setting out small plates on which to put the slices. Eris smiled, watching her work. "I can remember the first girl Ares liked," she remarked. "She looked a lot like you, actually. Pretty. Golden hair and all that."

Aphrodite raised an eyebrow at Ares. "Really? Tell me more," she said in a teasing, but intrigued tone.

"Nothing to tell," he protested quickly. "I was only three at the time. That girl and I were in the same temple daycare. Totally little kid stuff." He waved his hand as if to brush away that topic of conversation. And then he craned his neck over Aphrodite's shoulder to stare hungrily at the cake. "That looks great," he said.

As he'd hoped, Aphrodite dropped a big slice onto one of the small silver plates and handed it to him.

He wanted to tell her how pleased he was at all the trouble she'd gone to in planning this party, how much he appreciated and liked her. But he'd never been any good at "mushy" talk. And he especially didn't want to say all that in front of Eris and the guys.

Suddenly, Eris reached toward the plate of cake Ares held. "Thanks. I'd love some," she said. With lightning-quick reflexes, she snatched his plate away before he could even utter a protest. Typical. She'd often done stuff like that when they were growing up. She tore off a large hunk of the cake and stuffed it into her mouth.

He knew better than to try to get his plate back. Though Eris might look kind of scrawny, her appearance was deceptive. He absolutely did *not* want to provoke her if he could help it. He just hoped that no one else would, either.

Aphrodite was looking horrified at Eris's manners, or lack thereof, as were several of the other students standing near enough to have seen what had happened. "Yes, well, I'm glad you like it," she told Eris politely. Quickly, she cut a second piece of cake, this one even bigger. She slid it onto another silver plate and handed it to Ares. "Here you go, birthday boy!" she told him, grinning widely as if to make up for his sister's behavior.

"It's nice you could come to celebrate Ares's big day," she told Eris, as more cake was cut and handed around.

"Wouldn't have missed it for the world," Eris replied. She swallowed a bite of cake; then a gleam quite familiar to Ares came into her eyes. She stared at Aphrodite. "Hey," she said. "I just remembered something."

Uh-oh, he thought. From the calculating look in her eyes, he could tell that his sister was about to do something . . . disruptive. He tensed and stepped closer to Aphrodite, ready to protect her from whatever horrible thing Eris was about to say or do next.

She cocked her head at Aphrodite. "You're the

goddess who came from sea foam, right? The one with no parents?" she asked innocently.

The students standing nearby gasped, and Ares saw Aphrodite's shoulders stiffen. His fists clenched, and he frowned at his sister, boiling mad. But Eris hardly noticed. Her tongue darted out to lick frosting from her fingers. "Mm. Tasty," she murmured.

"Yep, that's me," Aphrodite replied after a few tense seconds. "Sea foam girl." Her overly bright voice told Ares that Eris had struck her where it hurt. She'd targeted his crush's feelings and hit the bull's-eye, just as she'd intended.

A secretive smile flitted across Eris's face and she shrugged slightly. "Yeah, I thought that must be you."

"Wow! This cake you made is *sooo* good, Aphrodite," Persephone rushed to say. She, Athena, and Artemis had slipped closer, coming to lend support.

"It's delish," Athena put in enthusiastically.

"Is there enough for seconds?" Artemis asked quickly, holding out her empty cake plate.

Ares was grateful that Aphrodite's three best friends had spoken up, attempting to distract her and everyone else.

Even Medusa came to Aphrodite's defense. She and the twelve snakes on top of her head were all scowling at his sister. In spite of the fact that Medusa—in her meaner days—used to call Aphrodite "Bubbles" because of the whole sea foam thing!

The snakes started hissing. Too bad Eris was immortal, Ares thought. Because if she were a mortal, and if she looked directly into Medusa's eyes right now, she would instantly turn to stone! Medusa's snake hair gave her that power, although most of the time she wore stoneglasses, which kept her from accidentally turning mortals to stone. Anyway, Eris wasn't looking at the snake-haired girl. She was staring straight at Aphrodite, seemingly unaware of anyone else.

"Sure, um, plenty for seconds," Aphrodite said in answer to Artemis's earlier question. Bending, she sliced more sections of cake.

"So, Eris," Persephone said quickly, sliding to stand between Eris and Aphrodite. "How much younger than Ares are you?"

Ares knew she was only trying to fix the damage Eris had done by introducing a new topic. Eris's petite stature had obviously confused her, as it did most people meeting his sister for the first time. Persephone had a knack for smoothing over awkward situations, but he wished she'd picked a different topic.

"Oh, I'm not younger. I'm his big sister. By eleven months," Eris crowed.

Ares winced. All his life, she'd constantly reminded him of that fact. She'd also used her superior age as justification for why she should always get first choice in everything they had or did. And why she could boss him around.

The gleam was back in her eyes now as she grabbed another slice of cake and dug in. "Remember when we were kids, Ares?" she asked between bites. "How we'd play that game where I was the Great and Magnificent Goddess of the Temple and your job was to be the mortal servant bearing gifts and following my orders? Good times." She smiled happily at the recollection.

Ares could only groan as the students around them laughed.

"Yeah, it's cool to grow up with a brother close to your age," said Artemis. "Like Apollo and me. Only we're twins." She gestured toward her brother, who, having just put away his lyre, had left the makeshift stage.

Eris sent Artemis a curious look. "Apollo's your brother? And you *both* go to school here?" she asked.

Artemis nodded. "That's right."

Whack! Eris banged her plate and fork down on the table next to her, her eyes narrowing at Ares. "You told me it was a rule that only one kid per family could attend MOA."

"Oh! Um," he sputtered. Apparently Eris had never read about Apollo and Artemis being twins in *Teen Scrollazine.* But now she knew he'd lied about that rule to keep her from trying to enroll at the Academy. Before he could reply, she spotted someone bending over the black bag she'd left beside the cupola door.

"Hey! Whose bag is this?" the bag-snooper called out. It was Pandora, a mortal MOA student who'd just arrived at the party.

"Leave that alone. It's mine!" Eris shouted, bounding over to grab her bag.

"Whoa! Did you think I was going to take it or something?" Pandora protested. Straightening away from it, she brushed back her question-mark-shaped bangs, a symbol of her bottomless curiosity.

Ares didn't hear the rest of what they said because just then Artemis piped up. "Why did you tell your sister that?" she asked him.

"Yeah. There's no rule stopping brothers and sisters from going to MOA," said Apollo. He'd come over from the stage to snag some cake.

"Shh," Ares warned. He lowered his voice, shooting a worried glance at Eris even though she was way over by the door and therefore too far away to hear. "I told her that back when Principal Zeus invited me to MOA in first grade, so she wouldn't try to follow me here. I don't want her to enroll, but it'll make her mad if I say so."

Apollo cocked his head. "Yeah, I get it. Sisters can be a pain at times—no one knows that better than me." He sent Artemis a teasing look, and she bopped him lightly on the arm.

"Brothers, too," she added, grinning at him. Then her crush, Actaeon, called to her and she took off.

"Your sister can't be *that* bad," Apollo said, darting Ares a look between bites of cake.

Ares's eyebrows rose. "You have *no* idea. I mean, did Artemis ever lock you outside in your underwear? Right when a bunch of neighborhood kids were walking by? Or did she cut off your hair while you were sleeping? Or constantly climb like a monkey to pelt you with apples from the top of a tree?"

"God-dude!" Apollo said in shocked surprise. "Your sister did all that?"

Ares nodded. "I'm telling you, she's a real pain. Literally. Those apples hurt! And—"

"Happy birthday!" a voice boomed suddenly, cutting him off. Both boys turned to see Principal Zeus and Hera sweep grandly into the cupola.

At seven feet tall, Zeus towered over everyone in the room. His head with its wild red hair and beard swiveled this way and that as his piercing blue eyes sought out the birthday boy. Hera, whose thick, blond hair was styled high, noticed Ares right away and pointed him out.

"Over here!" Poseidon called at the same time. He and Apollo's roommate, Dionysus, had come to stand by Apollo and were grinning broadly, aiming their fingers at Ares.

Principal Zeus strode over in three giant steps. Then he reached out to pump Ares's hand in one of his own meaty paws. The gold bands that circled his wrist flashed in the last remaining rays of sunlight shining down through the cupola's open dome. "So you're what now—fifteen, Ares?" Zeus asked.

"Uh, yeah. Something like that," Ares mumbled, not wanting to correct him. Contradicting Zeus was unwise at best. Besides, Ares felt kind of proud that Zeus thought he was older than he really was. Especially since the principal usually *under*estimated the ages of students, thinking of them as much younger than they actually were. And he often forgot names, but he'd remembered Ares's. Score! All of that was a birthday present in itself. But then Zeus reached into the pocket of his tunic and pulled out a small rectangular package neatly wrapped in shiny purple paper and tied with an elegant silver ribbon.

"Got something for you," he said. "Hera wrapped it,"

he added. Which is what Ares had already guessed. Zeus didn't "do" neat. Or gift wrapping. If it had been up to Zeus—to most guys Ares knew, as a matter of fact—he probably wouldn't have bothered with wrapping paper at all.

Ares tore open the paper to reveal a book. He read its title aloud: "*Winning at Capture the Flag and Other War Games.* Mega-cool! Thanks!" he proclaimed, genuinely pleased. "I'm training for the Temple Games. This book will be a big help."

"Principal Zeus? Hi!" Eris had come over and now somehow managed to insert herself between Zeus and Ares.

"Ow!" Ares protested when the contents of the bag she held jabbed his elbow. Whatever she had in there, it was hard and lumpy.

Zeus's bushy red eyebrows rose as he glanced down

at the girl. He frowned. "And who are . . .?" he started to ask.

"This is Eris, Ares's sister," Hera said warmly, coming to stand beside the girl. "She was in my shop at the Immortal Marketplace only yesterday, and I realized she didn't know about the party." Hera's shop, Hera's Happy Endings, sold dresses, decorations, and supplies for weddings. "I just assumed her invitation must've gotten lost in Hermes' delivery chariot," she explained. "So I invited her. All's well that ends well."

Mystery solved, thought Ares. He couldn't blame Hera for her mistake in thinking he might welcome his sister here.

Eris beamed at Hera before turning toward him. "I was at the Immortal Marketplace looking for a birthday present for you, *dear* brother," she said sweetly. She hugged the black bag in her arms.

Huh? he thought. If there was a gift inside it for him, he didn't want it.

"She's never given me a present in her life," he muttered to Apollo from one side of his mouth when Eris began talking to Hera again. "Unless you count the dog poop she gave me when I was three. Told me it was candy."

"Seriously?" said Apollo, looking rather shocked.

"Yeah," said Ares. "Luckily, I wasn't dumb enough to believe her." He watched Eris warily as she chatted up Zeus and Hera. "Then there was the cape she gave me when I was five," he went on to Apollo, speaking in a lowered voice so others wouldn't overhear. "It said KICK ME on the back of it."

At that Apollo burst out laughing.

"It wasn't funny!" Ares chided. "I couldn't read yet, so it got me into plenty of fights with older boys who could."

"They kicked you?"

"Not more than once," Ares told him, arching a brow.

When Zeus and Hera looked away from his sister to answer a question from Pandora, Dionysus spoke to Eris, his violet eyes teasing. "You were shopping for a birthday gift for Ares in a *wedding* shop?" Ares and Poseidon heard him ask.

Poseidon let out a snort and glanced toward Aphrodite, who was heading for Zeus and Hera with two plates of cake. "Yeah! That's kind of rushing things, don't you think, Eris?" Twirling his trident—he carried the three-pronged spear almost everywhere—the turquoise godboy laughed.

Following his gaze, Eris laughed, too.

Ares could feel his cheeks warm. "Ha!" he said, to cover his embarrassment at the teasing. One of the spear decorations had come loose from a column, and he picked it up, testing its blunt point.

Having overheard, Hera smiled over at him indulgently. "When your sister explained who she was and told me she hadn't seen you in a long time, we decided that the best present she could give you was the gift of her presence."

At that, Zeus frowned a little. Hera didn't seem to notice, but all the students standing close enough to see the thunder gather in his face looked nervous. Ares wondered if they should run for cover. Invitations to visit MOA always came through Zeus. *Always.* Didn't Hera know that?

It was probably a good thing Aphrodite arrived with the cake just then. "Mmm, *chocolate!*" Zeus exclaimed, his eyes lighting up like a little kid's. "My favorite!"

Hera took a small bite of her piece and pronounced it delicious. "You don't mind that I invited Eris here, do you, dear?" she asked him in a concerned voice that suggested she knew she'd violated a rule but expected him to back her up just this once.

Buoyed by the birthday cake, Zeus rose to the occasion. "No, it's fine, honeybun." Making his voice louder, he said, "I'll make an exception for you and you only." His piercing blue eyes swept the room so that everyone would know that he meant it.

"Thanks so much!" Eris said sweetly, her voice dripping with nectar. Clutching her black bag tightly, she bounced on her toes. "I'm so excited to be here!"

Zeus and others around them sent her smiles, but she didn't fool Ares. He didn't trust her. Not one little bit. However, it looked like he'd have to put up with his annoying sister until the party was over. He wasn't sure how much longer it was supposed to last, but probably no more than a couple of hours. He hoped!

3

Party Games

Aphrodite

PRINCIPAL ZEUS?"

Aphrodite twisted around to see that Ms. Hydra, the principal's nine-headed administrative assistant, had come looking for him. Each of her heads was a different color and had a different personality.

"You wanted me to let you know when those semester-end grades were on your desk?" her efficient gray head said as it poked through the cupola door on its long neck. "Well, they're in."

"Excellent!" boomed Zeus. "I'll come take a look at them." Grabbing a silver plate with a second piece of cake, he abruptly headed out the door. As he passed Ms. Hydra, her cheerful yellow head peered around the edge of the door beside her gray one. "Ooh, a party! How nice!" it said.

"It's Ares's birthday," Aphrodite told her as the other seven of her nine heads bobbled in the background, each craning to get a look at the decorations.

"Happy birthday, Ares!" they all chorused. Some of the voices were upbeat, others grumpy or impatient, depending on which head it was.

"Thanks, Ms. Hydra," Ares called back, waving a toy spear Aphrodite had just noticed him holding. However, his eyes were glued to Eris, and there was something odd in his tone, thought Aphrodite. In fact, ever since his sister had arrived, he'd been acting weird. What was up?

"Wait! Take some cake back to the office with you," she called out as Ms. Hydra started to follow the principal. Aphrodite hurried over to the table to grab a plate with the biggest slice she could find, since she figured that all nine heads would be sharing it. Ms. Hydra's yellow head thanked her delightedly.

"Nice of you to give her some cake before she *headed off*," Persephone said from beside her. Aphrodite smiled at her silly joke, but her mind was still puzzling over Ares's behavior.

Grr! Grr! Sss!

What now? she wondered. Looking past a group of students, she saw that Hera, who hadn't left with Zeus, was chatting with Athena, who was her stepdaughter, of course. And Ares's sister had gone over to talk with Artemis and Medusa. Oddly, Artemis's three dogs and Medusa's snakes seemed as wary of Eris as Adonis had been. The dogs growled while edging away from the petite girl, then ran to Apollo with their tails tucked between their legs. And Medusa's snakes were rearing back, as far away from Eris as possible. Eyeing her nervously, they had begun to hiss.

A strong hand fell on Aphrodite's arm, pulling her aside. She looked up. Ares had come over. "Hey, um . . . about my sister," he started to say.

He looked so apologetic and worried that Aphrodite suddenly realized what must be going on. He was acting weird because he was worried Eris had hurt her feelings earlier with the sea foam thing. That had to be it. *How sweet of him!*

Before he could continue, she interrupted. "Not

too tactful, is she? But that's okay. I'm sure she didn't mean to hurt my feelings before."

Eris glanced over at them just then, and her eyes glinted. Before Ares could say anything more, the girl called out, "Hey, Aphrodite, how about a party game?"

"Sure," Aphrodite agreed as murmurs of interest ran through the partygoers. "Any suggestions?" she asked the room. "Pin the Tail on the Trojan Horse? Ten in a Temple? MOA-opoly?"

"I'm game for anything," Persephone announced. She and her crush, Hades, were over by the snacks table now, munching on chips. "Except Truth or Dare," she added quickly. Her GGBFFs laughed. They knew she was probably thinking about a recent "dare" that had taken her way out of her comfort zone and landed her onstage at the mega-popstar Orpheus's Rock the Gods concert!

"How about Two Truths and a Lie?" Eris suggested.

Ares groaned aloud.

"Sounds like fun," Aphrodite said quickly, elbowing him gently in the ribs. Even though Eris had hurt *her* feelings, Aphrodite hoped his groan hadn't hurt *Eris's* feelings.

"Ooh," Pheme said excitedly. Words puffed above her head as she went on. "I love that game. Everyone in our chariot played it on the way to that journalism conference we went to. Remember, Eros?"

"Wait—" Ares tried to butt in.

"Oh, yeah," said Eros, before he could finish. "The game where you have to say three statements about yourself—two that are true, and one that's a lie, right?"

"Right. Then everyone has to guess which one's the lie," Eris explained to the room in general. "You eliminate players with the fewest points at the end of each round until there's just one winner left."

"Sounds thrilling," Apollo said, making a face. "I vote for Pin the Tail on the Trojan Horse. Who's with me?" He uttered a magic spell that instantly produced a three-foot-tall flat cut-out drawing of a wooden horse. In his hand he now held a tail to match.

"Great idea," seconded Dionysus. "Anybody got a blindfold?"

All the boys eagerly fell in with Apollo's idea instead of Eris's. Artemis and a few other girls did, too. Ares was the only boy to hesitate, his gaze switching back and forth between Eris and Apollo.

"Go on," Aphrodite urged him. "I know you'd rather wear a pink chiton to your war games competition than play Two Truths and a Lie. You love Pin the Tail on the Trojan Horse, so go. It's your birthday. Have fun!" She gave him a gentle push in the direction of his friends, and the crowd divided up, each group heading to opposite sides of the room. Oddly enough, Apollo had to practically drag Ares off to get him to go with the rest of the guys.

"Let's get in a circle. It's easier to play that way," Pheme eagerly suggested. Aphrodite and the other girls grabbed chairs. Meanwhile, the other group began to play the Pin the Tail game across the room. Aphrodite watched their big paper horse snort and stamp its hooves, preparing to run from whoever was blindfolded first. And that was apparently going to be Ares. His friends were laughing and saying that the birthday boy should get first try.

"Where's my bag?" Eris blurted suddenly, drawing her attention.

"Oh!" gasped Hera at almost the same time. "Here it is." She'd been making her way toward the cupola door as if ready to leave, when she'd tripped over that very bag. She picked it up, holding it upside down. Something golden and gleaming started to slide out, and she grabbed it before it could fall.

Eris rushed over and snatched her bag away. "Thanks. I'll take that," she said, pushing the golden object back inside. As Eris rejoined the girls in the quickly forming circle of chairs, Hera just stood there gazing after her with a strange expression of longing on her face.

"So what's the prize for the winner?" Pandora asked Eris.

"Glad you asked," Eris replied. Pushing her chair between the ones Athena and Aphrodite had positioned close together, she opened her bag. And pulled out . . . a trophy! Its top was a highly polished golden apple that sat upon a slender vertical gold rod, which connected it to a square base. The whole trophy was only about ten inches tall.

What a weird thing to carry around, thought Aphrodite. She and Athena traded looks from where they sat on either side of Eris. From the expression on her face, Athena obviously thought it was strange, too. *But, whatever.* Eris was Ares's sister. So Aphrodite was determined to overlook the girl's oddities and be friends with her.

Hearing a sudden cheer from the other group across the room, she glanced over and saw that the blindfolded Ares was really into the game now. He'd just lunged and missed the Trojan horse and was after it again.

"Here, take a closer look," she heard Eris say to someone. Aphrodite swung back around in her seat. There was a gleam almost as bright as gold in Eris's eyes as she held out the trophy to Athena.

"Okay," said Athena. As a few more girls brought chairs over to their circle, she took the trophy politely but without enthusiasm. However, as she held it, her face slowly lit up. "Wow! It's lovely. Really beautiful," she said avidly. Gripping its base in one hand, she cupped the golden apple in her other. "In fact, it's the most beautiful trophy I've ever seen!"

"I agree. It's so smooth. So perfectly shaped," another voice gushed. It was Hera's. She seemed to have changed her mind about leaving the party. Instead, she brought a chair over to the group and sat on Athena's other side, two over from Aphrodite.

"I know!" Athena agreed. "The apple looks so real!"

Aphrodite stared at them in surprise. Hello? It was just a trophy. No better and no worse than most other trophies, as far as she could see. Why were these two acting so mega-bizarro over it? The Hera she knew was pleasant and warm, but no-nonsense. If there was one thing Hera was not, it was a goddess who gushed! And the brainy Athena was usually levelheaded and not at all prone to exaggeration. She'd won tons of awards, including having the city of Athens named after her when she invented the olive. So why would Athena get so excited over this simple trophy?

Hera gazed around the circle. "You girls don't mind if I join your game, do you?"

Eris looked a little nervous about this, but Aphrodite jumped in and said, "Sure. Have a seat." Of course, Hera had already seated herself.

Eris reached to take back her trophy. "Here, let Aphrodite see it," she told Athena.

Athena frowned a little, hugging the trophy to her chest. But then she seemed to realize how odd a thing that was to do and reluctantly passed the trophy to Eris, who then thrust it into Aphrodite's hands.

"Oh, um, thanks. Yeah, it's very . . . ," Aphrodite said,

nodding. Suddenly, she sucked in a sharp breath as the trophy's true beauty abruptly became apparent to her as well. She'd only intended to examine it quickly and hand it right back. Because, really, who cared about a trophy if they hadn't won it? But as soon as she clasped this one, it suddenly became clear to her why Hera and Athena had been so enchanted by it.

"Ye gods," she said in wonderment. "It really *is* magnificent!" She glided her fingertips over the gleaming, shiny gold apple. On the base of the trophy she noticed words. Tipping it closer, she read them in a soft voice. "For the Fairest." Her heart beat faster. Surely that must mean the trophy was meant to be hers. She was the goddessgirl of love and *beauty* after all. And *fairest* meant most beautiful, right? Not that she was vain about her looks, of course. But still . . .

"Can we start the game now? And, hey, where

did you get that trophy?" she heard the ever-curious Pandora ask Eris. "Did you win it for apple picking or something?"

Eris answered only one of the three questions. "I bought it from that Be a Hero store in the Immortal Marketplace, after I went to Hera's shop yesterday. The shopkeeper promised me it was one of a kind."

"You mean, Mr. Dolos?" asked Medusa, with a disgusted snort. "That guy's a liar and a cheat!" But then she shrugged. "He's a good businessman, though. He used to have just the one store near my hometown on the Aegean coast. His second store in the IM is a big step up."

Mr. Dolos had once paid Medusa for the use of her image, Aphrodite recalled. But then he'd altered it in an unflattering way and used it on a toy shield he falsely advertised as magic. A short round man with slicked-back hair and a stiffly curled mustache, he usually dressed in a tacky bright yellow-and-black checkered tunic. Medusa was probably right about him. After all, Aphrodite figured, how could anyone with such poor taste in fashion be reliable?

Persephone was sitting on Aphrodite's other side and reached for the trophy. "Can I see it?"

"No!" When Aphrodite pulled back so she couldn't touch it, Persephone looked startled and a little hurt. And now the other girls around the circle were looking at Aphrodite like she'd flipped her lid. But who cared? she thought as the trophy hypnotized her with its dreamy, gleaming magnificence. She couldn't bear to let it go. And what's more, she felt an overwhelming impulse to win the game they were going to play so she could possess it forever.

Without warning, Eris snatched the trophy away from her.

"Hey!" Aphrodite protested, feeling like she'd just lost her best golden, gleaming friend.

Eris ignored her and gazed around the circle of girls (and Hera) who were now sitting in the chairs. "Pandora's right. Let's get this game started!" she said.

Just then Ares and Apollo came over. Seeing them, Eris frowned and quickly jammed the trophy into her black bag. "What are you doing here?"

"We got kicked out of our game early," said Ares.

"Yeah, I've never seen Ares play so lame," Apollo added, looking confused. "I mean it! It was like he *wanted* to lose. He was so far off the mark that he almost pinned his tail on *me*!"

"Huh? Slight exaggeration," Ares said with a fake laugh. "Anyway, can we play with you guys?" When some girls scooched over to make room, he dragged over two chairs and sat in one. Apollo plopped into the other, sending Ares a perplexed "what's up with you?" glance.

"Whatever, birthday boy," said Eris. She seemed suddenly intent on getting the game going. Glancing around the circle, she said, "So who's first?"

Hera rubbed her hands together. "I'll start."

"Humph!" Aphrodite and Athena both snorted.

What was Hera thinking, barging into their game like this? wondered Aphrodite. This was a *student* party. Grown-ups always put a damper on student fun. Besides, why would she suddenly want to hang out with them?

"Okay, here goes. My two truths and a lie," Hera began cheerfully. "I taught Zeus how to dance. I dye my hair. I'm not allergic to feathers."

Aphrodite was pretty sure Hera's first statement was true since Zeus's dancing had improved right after he and Hera had begun seeing each other. And she was also pretty sure that Hera was not allergic to feathers since she had a chariot drawn by peacocks and sometimes wore peacock feathers in her hair. So the hair dye statement must be the lie. Which made sense because her hair color looked natural.

As they went around the circle, all but three people guessed correctly that the hair dye was the lie. Score one point for those who'd guessed right, and three points to Hera who got one point from each player who had guessed wrong.

Now it was Pandora's turn. "Are my favorite colors red and green? Do I love questions? Do I have a Magic Answer Ball?"

"Uh, those are questions," said Eris. She thought for a second and then said, "So everyone can just try to pick the one that should be answered no."

That was easy. As everyone knew, Pandora's favorite colors were blue and gold—MOA's official colors and the color of her hair, too. So Pandora got nothing and everyone else got one point. More players went, and then it was Apollo's turn.

After thinking a few seconds, he said, "I can see the future. I have a twin sister. I don't like pythons."

"God-dude." Ares groaned from beside him. "*All* of those are true."

Apollo shrugged, grinning. "Well, I'm the godboy of truth. I *can't* tell a lie."

"No points for you, then," Eris huffed, frowning at him. "And one point goes to everyone else."

Ares took the next turn. "My trident has four prongs. I can't swim. I invented the olive."

Aphrodite stared at him, as did everyone else. "Tridents have *three* prongs. Besides that, you don't own one," she said.

"And you *can* swim," noted Apollo.

"And *I* invented the olive," Athena added.

"So those are *all* lies," said Aphrodite, smiling bemusedly at her crush's oddball sense of humor. "Plus they're things Poseidon would say."

Ares grinned at her. "I guess Apollo can't lie and *I* can't tell the truth," he quipped.

It wasn't really true. Still, it was funny and everyone laughed. Except Eris, that is. She grew red in the face and stamped her foot. "Some of you are not taking this game seriously!" she snapped.

Whoa, thought Aphrodite. Apparently, Eris had a hot temper to rival the one Ares *used* to have. Growing up with someone like her, it was easy to see where he might have gotten his competitive spirit.

After Eris's outburst, players seemed to try harder to follow the rules. But it was pretty easy to guess the lies they came up with. Medusa's, for example, was, "I'm immortal." Even someone meeting her for the very first time would know that was a lie, since immortals had skin that shimmered. Hers was green and definitely did not.

Athena fooled quite a few people with her lie, however. It was, "I've never gone to see the Gray Ladies." Because she was smart, most people couldn't imagine her ever needing to talk to the Gray Ladies, who were the school counselors. Still, the ladies didn't just advise students about academic matters.

Athena's three BFFs, plus Medusa, Pandora, and Hera, were the only ones who knew that Athena had once gone to see the counselors to talk over her feelings about Zeus getting married again. (This was after her mom—who was an actual buzzy fly named Metis—had literally decided to fly away from Mount Olympus!)

It was very crafty of Athena to risk such a personal statement that few in the game could've guessed, thought Aphrodite. Look at all the points she'd earned!

Eris refused a turn, so Aphrodite was the last to go. "My favorite color is pink," she said. *Oops. Too easy,* she thought when everyone laughed. She smoothed a hand over the hem of her cotton-candy-pink chiton, and thought harder. After a few seconds, she added, "I can make armpit farts. I get mostly A's on my report cards."

There, she thought. *Those two will confuse a lot of people.* It was true that she mostly got all A's, but many students seemed to think that beauty and brains couldn't go together. As for the armpit farts, few would imagine her ever doing anything so crass. However, she'd actually armpit-played goofy songs while under the spell of a "rude" trouble bubble that had escaped from a box Pandora had once gotten ahold of. Mortified when she learned what she'd done after the bubble's enchantment had worn off, Aphrodite had sworn everyone who knew to secrecy.

She peeked over at Ares now to see him grinning widely. She'd never told him about her special "talent." It didn't fit the image of her she wanted him to have. But if Athena could admit that she'd been to see the counselors, then *she* could admit to making fart noises. That was how badly both of them wanted the trophy!

Turned out that her strategy worked. Only Pandora, Athena, and Persephone guessed correctly. Artemis knew, too, but she was off playing the Pin the Tail game.

"So who won?" asked Aphrodite once the game ended.

Eris quickly added up the points, but Athena was faster, doing it in her head. "The front-runners are Aphrodite and me."

"Front-runners?" Aphrodite echoed.

"Since the scores between the two of you are so close, I think it's only fair to play one more round," said Eris.

"Then let's do it," said Athena.

"Sorry, I have to take off," Persephone apologized, getting to her feet. "I told my mom I'd be home by eight and I'm already late." Unlike most MOA girls, she lived with her mother, the goddess Demeter, most of the time and commuted by winged sandal to school each day. She handed Adonis to Aphrodite for a quick farewell hug. Since it was Persephone's week to take care of him, the kitten would be going home with her.

"I'll miss you, cutie patootie," Aphrodite told the kitten, giving it a pet. It was dark by now, she realized. Some players had left their chairs to begin cleaning up the cupola. A few had even drifted off to their dorm rooms to finish homework assignments before getting ready for bed. The Pin the Tail game had just ended too. She'd been so focused on the Two Truths and a Lie game that she hadn't even heard them running around on the other side of the room as they played.

"I'll take you home in my chariot," she heard Hades tell Persephone. As the two of them exited through the cupola door, Ares stood up from his chair and stretched. "Don't you think you'd better be getting home too?" he hinted to Eris. "It's getting late. I say we declare this game a tie and call it a night."

Aphrodite and Athena looked at each other in alarm. Hera looked upset too. Did she really think she was still in the running? Her scores from the first round were so low there was no way she could catch up. It struck Aphrodite then that all three of them equally yearned to possess the magnificent apple trophy. What was it about that trophy that drew them so? She didn't care. She only knew that *she* was going to be the one to get it.

Before Eris could respond to Ares's suggestion, Zeus reappeared in the cupola. He was already dressed in slippers, a dark blue velvety robe, and pj's that had a blue and yellow thunderbolt design. "You're still here, Hera?" he said with a big yawn.

Hera flashed a covetous glance at the bag on the floor by Eris's chair. The one that held the precious golden apple trophy. "We were playing a game," she told Zeus. "There's one more round to go. I'll be along after I've won."

Aphrodite couldn't believe it. Hera really didn't seem to get that she'd already lost. Or maybe she only refused to accept it.

Athena gave her stepmom a twisted smile. "I believe *I'm* ahead."

What? thought Aphrodite. Her stomach clenched. *She* was the fairest, so obviously the trophy was meant for her! "You mean *we* are ahead. In a tie."

Athena just shrugged.

Looking a little befuddled, Zeus glanced from his wife to his daughter, then back again to Hera. "Come on, sugar pie," he coaxed. "The game can't be that important."

Hera pouted, flicking her hands at him in a shooing motion. "Go. I'm staying," she declared.

Uh-oh, thought Aphrodite. She was sure that Hera had gone too far this time. Zeus didn't like to be defied. By anyone. Even though she'd never seen him get mad at Hera, Aphrodite cringed, fully expecting him to rain thunderbolts down upon them all.

To her surprise, he was uncharacteristically patient. And crafty, too. He turned to Ares. "I imagine your sister needs to get home. Why don't you see her on her way?"

Ares leaped out of his chair. "Good idea!"

"No. Wait!" Aphrodite, Hera, and Athena chorused.

"I'm scared of the dark!" Eris announced before they could continue. All eyes swung to her. "And I'm sooo tired. Can't I sleep over at MOA tonight?" She yawned a big fake-looking yawn, probably trying to convince Zeus.

He frowned. "Don't you need to get back for school tomorrow?"

"It's my school's semester break," Eris rushed to say. "Two weeks off."

Athena jumped up. "Yes! Let her stay, Dad. Then we can at least finish the game tomorrow. We were really having fun. Please?"

"All right," Zeus agreed, softening in the face of her beseeching. Aphrodite had the feeling that he was still reluctant to let Eris linger here at MOA, however.

"Yes!" Hera crowed. She got to her feet, clasping her hands together in delight. But then a fretful look came into her eyes and her shoulders slumped. "Wait. I just remembered I have a big shipment of gowns coming to my shop tomorrow. And appointments all week. I'll have to leave early in the morning for the IM."

"Oh, too bad, sweetcakes," Zeus said. Not looking

sorry at all, he took Hera's elbow and steered her toward the cupola door.

"But I wanted to win the trophy," Hera protested as she and Zeus neared the exit.

"Trophy? What trophy? You've already got the best trophy any woman could ever hope to win," he told her. "You've got *me!*"

To Hera's credit, she laughed. "True," she said fondly. Then the two of them headed off.

Aphrodite's spirits brightened. With Hera out of the competition, she had a fifty-fifty chance of winning Eris's glorious golden trophy. But Athena was smiling too. Was she thinking the same thing?

"Wait!" Eris piped up just as Zeus followed Hera out the door. "Could I maybe stay longer than just tonight? Like maybe a couple of days? Or a week?"

Zeus turned back, his eyebrows slamming together.

Sparks of electricity zinged from his fingers and crackled in the air around him, a sure sign he was annoyed.

"It's just that I hardly ever get to see Ares," Eris mumbled. Aphrodite gasped softly. Eris was really pushing her luck.

"But where would you stay?" Ares put in. "And what'll you do all day while we have classes? It'll be boring. So maybe it would be better if you go on ho —"

He broke off as Eris sniffled. A little crocodile tear slid down her cheek. Aphrodite was pretty sure it was fake, since it had happened so quickly. Ares didn't look taken in either, but the tear seemed to totally fool Zeus.

"Are you . . . *crying*?" he asked in horrified tones. He started backing toward the door, where Hera still lingered, his blue eyes wide now. "Stop. It's okay. I hereby proclaim that you can stay till dinner tomorrow."

Eris nodded meekly. "You're so kind," she whispered.

"Yeah," Zeus said gruffly. Then he drew himself up into a regal pose, turned abruptly, and marched from the cupola with Hera on his arm. Only the King of the Gods and Ruler of the Heavens could make an exit in thunderbolt pj's still look dignified, thought Aphrodite.

"Why are you and Athena so keen on that trophy?" a voice asked from beside her. Pandora.

"I don't know. It's cute, that's all," Aphrodite told her, though that wasn't really it. She wasn't sure she could explain her attraction to the trophy in a way that would make sense to anyone else.

Her eyes went longingly to the black trophy bag on the floor. She noticed that Athena was looking at it as well. That girl might be smart, but *she* could be smart, too! And she was going to do everything in her power to make sure that the fabulous trophy wound up hers!

4
An Accident

Ares

ERIS SEEMED QUITE PLEASED WITH HERSELF
for finagling an extra day at MOA, thought Ares as he
and Apollo unwound the final remaining silver ribbon
from a column. A bunch of students had stayed behind
to help when the party ended, and now the decorations
were down and the cake stuff had been cleaned up.
All that was left to do was to stash the boxes of deco-

rations in the storage cupboards along the wall.

"That's the last of the streamers," he told Aphrodite. "Thanks again for a great party. It was so—"

"Uh-huh. Sure," she said, cutting him off. "Hey, Eris," she called out. "Want to sleep over in my room tonight? I've got a spare bed."

Ares groaned. But before he could utter a protest, Eris called back from across the room, "Sure, love to!"

Great. The last thing he needed was for his sister to get chummy with his crush. From the corner of one eye, he saw Athena shoot Aphrodite a dark look. *Uh-oh*, he thought. Looked like Eris was having her usual effect on others. Those two goddessgirls typically got along great. And Aphrodite had been rude to him just now, which wasn't like her. Both were due to the influence of his troublemaking sister, no doubt.

"Sharing your room with my sister is a bad idea,"

Ares told Aphrodite in a quiet voice as they began to stow the boxes of decorations. "Come up with some reason you just remembered why you can't, okay?"

"Ha!" she teased, smiling at him. "You're just afraid she'll tell me some things about you that you don't want me to know." She shoved a box of streamers onto a low shelf in one of the storage cupboards.

Ares slid the heavier one he was carrying into an empty space on a higher shelf. "That's not it at all," he insisted, though that wasn't strictly true. There *were* some stories Eris could tell that he'd just as soon Aphrodite didn't hear. Like the embarrassing ones he'd told Apollo. "You don't know what she's like," he went on, keeping his voice low so that no one else—especially not Eris—would hear. "Truth is . . . she's the goddess of strife and discord!"

"And you're the godboy of war," Aphrodite

reminded him, shrugging. "If I can get along with you, I'm pretty sure I can get along with your sister."

Ares didn't know how to respond to that. After all, she had a point. When she went to fetch another boxful of decorations from the center of the room, he followed. His mind raced as he tried to think of another way to convince her not to let Eris spend the night, but he came up empty.

With everyone's help, all the boxes were soon neatly stowed away, except for one that someone had stuffed full of Ares's birthday presents. Although it was heavy, he hefted it easily onto one shoulder to carry up to his room. He and Aphrodite walked side by side toward the exit door along with the other students who had stayed to help tidy up.

All smiles now, Eris pushed her way between Aphrodite and him, linking arms with Aphrodite. She still had that black bag of hers. She'd been guarding it for some reason instead of helping with the cleanup. Was there a birthday present inside it for him, or not? he wondered. Probably best not to bring it up, since any gift from her would probably be something intended to embarrass or wound him.

"MOA is fantastic," Eris said, gazing out one of the cupola windows at the moonlit statues and the golden fountain in the courtyard below as the two girls started out ahead of him. "Wouldn't it be great if I could go to school here, too?"

"Yeah, I don't know why Zeus hasn't invited you already!" Aphrodite agreed readily.

Behind them, Ares rolled his eyes. He couldn't think of anything *worse* than having his sister here all the time. Luckily, Principal Zeus was not dumb. He must know Eris was the goddess of discord. The fact that he'd hesitated to let her stay seemed to show that he'd already figured out she was trouble. No way he'd invite her to enroll as an MOA student. Right?

The rest of the students were ahead of them by now. The last one to leave, Ares blew out the candles and shut the cupola door. After going down the winding stairs, he, his crush, and his sister were soon out on the main floor of the Academy. From there they took the marble staircase up toward the dorms.

As they climbed the steps, Aphrodite asked Eris, "So where do you think Mr. Dolos got that cool trophy?"

"What trophy?" Ares asked.

"Oh, it's nothing," Eris said quickly. Then to Aphrodite she said, "What I want to know is where you got that awesome outfit."

"This?" Aphrodite replied, reaching to give the skirt of her chiton a little swish with one hand. "It's just something I whipped up myself actually." This sent the two off on a long-winded fashion discussion that Ares tuned out. Seemed like Aphrodite had totally forgiven Eris for her sea foam remark. It was nice of his crush to befriend his sister, but he feared her kindness wasn't worth the effort. Eris was better at *destroying* friendships than creating them.

He shifted the box of birthday gifts to his other shoulder. But then he almost dropped the box in alarm when Eris asked Aphrodite, "So how many brothers and sisters go to MOA anyway?"

"Well, there are Artemis and Apollo, of course," Aphrodite replied. "And the Gorgon sisters—Medusa, Stheno, and Euryale. They're triplets, only Medusa isn't immortal like her sisters are. She's the girl with the snaky hair, remem—"

"Yeah, yeah," interrupted Eris. "Zeus only allows

78

twins or triplets to attend MOA? Is that it? No just brothers and sisters like Ares and me?"

Ares's shoulders tensed. Was his lie about to be exposed? Eris went to Corinthian Middle School now, but it probably wouldn't last. Sooner or later, the strife and discord she brought with her would result in mayhem. And ultimately in her being expelled. And then . . .

"It's just that I'd love to go to school with Ares. Wouldn't that be fun?" As they all passed the third floor, Eris looked back over her shoulder at him and raised her brows as if daring him to disagree.

Ares just grunted, which caused Aphrodite to send him an annoyed look. She had no clue. All these years, the Academy had been his sanctuary, he wanted to tell her. A place where he was far away from Eris. Safe from her troublemaking powers. He knew it bugged his sister that he'd been here since first grade yet she was excluded. Well, tough. The good life he'd made for himself here at MOA was over if Principal Zeus ever invited her here.

"Hmm. I'm having trouble coming up with any brothers or sisters at MOA that aren't twins or triplets, come to think of it," Aphrodite said at last, her forehead wrinkled in thought.

Phew, thought Ares. Saved! Now Eris would keep thinking that the whole "MOA no-siblings rule" was true except in certain cases.

"You know, you should be careful about that," Eris said sweetly as she examined Aphrodite's expression.

"About what?" Aphrodite asked in confusion, since his sister's comment had come out of nowhere.

"Forehead wrinkles," Eris explained, her eyes on Aphrodite's face.

"Oh no. Was I wrinkling my forehead? I'm usually

very careful about that kind of thing," Aphrodite said with a note of alarm. Wrinkles were fine for anyone else, but since she was the goddess of beauty, Ares knew she believed she had an image to maintain! Automatically, her fingers went to her face, tracing nonexistent lines.

Eris nodded. "And now you're making frown wrinkles." She shook her head, *tsk*ing.

"You see them, don't you, Ares?" There was a tiny smile at the corners of his sister's mouth as she looked back at him, her eyes gleaming.

"Huh?" said Ares. As usual, Eris was trying to create conflict. He was used to her doing that. As the goddess of strife and discord, it was what she did best.

Aphrodite had paused on the second-floor landing, and her pretty face was tilted up at him now as she awaited his reply. He was cornered. No matter how he answered, he was sure to say the wrong thing. If he told

Aphrodite he saw no wrinkles, she'd accuse him of lying. If he said she did have a few, she'd get mad at him!

Why did girls worry so much about how they looked anyway? he wondered. Aphrodite was perfect. Didn't she know that? Her long golden hair gleamed in the light from the torches that lined the Academy walls. Her blue eyes sparkled. Her heart-shaped face never failed to turn him to mush. Ares blurted, "I think Aphrodite is gorgeous, inside and out." And that was the truth!

His crush sent him a sweet, grateful glance and linked her arm with his free one. Now he was between the girls as they started upward again. Score one for him. Take that, Eris! However, his sister looked ready with yet another barb that would likely cause more trouble.

Quickly he said something to redirect her attention, a favorite tactic of his that worked well with some girls, he'd found. "So how are things at home, sis?"

Sure enough, Eris forgot whatever she'd been about to say. With a huge sigh, she replied, "Mom's on the war-path. Again."

"What about?" Ares asked, genuinely interested. He darted a glance at Aphrodite and saw with relief that she seemed interested too. *Phew.* Looked like he was off the hook for any more of that "wrinkly" discussion.

His sister's face darkened and she clenched her fists. "Corinthian Middle School gave me the boot yesterday. Can you believe it?"

Her words formed a lump of dread in Ares's chest. So that's why she'd shown up at Hera's shop in the IM, he suddenly realized. It had nothing to do with his birthday. That was just an excuse. As he'd halfway suspected, it had really been the first step in her game plan to get an invitation to her dream school—MOA!

"How awful! You mean you were expelled?" asked Aphrodite. "Why?" she asked after Eris nodded.

"The principal blamed me for this stupid little accident that could've happened to anyone." She paused, then added more quietly, "Too bad, because I kind of liked it there." As soon as she said that last, she shot Ares an embarrassed glance, as if she thought confessing that had been an admission of weakness. And to her, it probably was!

He did a quick calculation. Eris had been kicked out of at least ten schools by now, he figured. It would be a huge mistake to mention that, though. If he did, sooner or later, she'd make him pay for bringing it up.

"What kind of accident?" Aphrodite asked.

"Well, I was acting as conflict-resolution monitor during recess," Eris began.

"What?" Ares let out a guffaw, and both girls shot

him exasperated glances. He was still trying to wrap his head around the idea of his sister being a *conflict-resolution* monitor as she went on.

"So I decided to help this group of kids settle their differences by holding a contest," said Eris. "To see who could build the world's largest snowman on the school roof."

Hearing this foolishness, Ares felt some of the old anger well up inside him.

"Oh, no! What happened?" Aphrodite asked, wide-eyed.

"Well, during the night, the roof of the school collapsed." Eris shrugged. "Who knew snow could be so heavy, right?"

"Ye gods!" Aphrodite exclaimed as they reached the fourth floor at last. "Was anyone hurt?"

"Nuh-uh. School was closed. Everyone was gone by then."

"What a dumb—and dangerous—thing to do!" Ares

blasted, for once not caring if Eris retaliated.

"Huh? You sound just like the principal!" she replied with a frown. "It wasn't my fault that roof was weak. Anyway, the school is out of commission for now. Seemed like the perfect time to come visit you, bro!"

Ares let out a huff. Steadying the box on his shoulder, he reached his free hand toward the door to the girls' dorm hall. He was more than ready to be rid of his sister for the night. He'd bet his favorite spear that she'd had something to do with causing the "differences" among those kids that she'd been "helping" at her school in the first place! She never thought anything was her fault. But once he told Zeus her story, there wouldn't be a snowball's chance in Hades's Underworld that he'd invite her to MOA, no matter how she begged. Which meant he was safe. The thought calmed him.

"In you go, Eris . . . ," he hinted, opening the door

and holding it wide. He needed to warn Aphrodite about her in private.

"Oh, but I was hoping you'd show me your room," Eris told him, refusing to budge. "Fifth floor, right?"

"Sorry," Ares said as he rebalanced his box of gifts again. "No girls allowed on the boys' hall and vice versa. The rules."

"Rules schmules," said Eris. Ignoring him, she rushed upstairs, heading for the boys' dorm hall one floor up.

"She can have a peek down your hall at least, can't she?" Aphrodite argued, as they followed his sister. "No harm in that."

Ares snorted. "Oh, really?" Eris could make trouble between two dust bunnies given half a chance.

Up on the fifth floor, she was already opening the door. "Hey! What's up, guys?" she called down the boys' hall.

"Eek!" It was Poseidon's voice, raised in alarm. Ares got there just in time to see him—in his fish-patterned pj's—racing down the hall from the bathroom to his room, his trident leaving a trail of water across the floor. Eris and Aphrodite both giggled, obviously amused.

Shifting the box of gifts to his hip, Ares grabbed the door from his sister and ducked his head inside. "Girls in the hall!" he yelled to warn the other guys. A few poked their heads out to look, then drew them back into their rooms like startled turtles retreating into their shells.

The two girls stared down the hall, looking fascinated for some reason. He followed their gazes, noticing stuff he didn't usually notice. The stuff he and the guys kept outside their doors, like various projects they were tinkering with. There was even a half-built chariot down near the room Apollo and Dionysus shared.

Random objects littered the hallway, like stray sandals, spears, clubs, javelins, archery bows, and Hero-ology class projects. It looked kind of messy, he guessed, but it worked for them!

Ares figured he'd be just as interested looking at the girls' hall as these girls were in the boys', but enough was enough. "Okay, show's over." He started to close the door.

Suddenly Eris pointed past it to the life-size suit of armor that stood outside his dorm room. The armored "knight" held a shield in one hand and a spear in the other. "I remember that!" she exclaimed.

Ares nodded. "Yeah, you helped me build it when we were kids." It was one of the few fond memories he had of her.

"I didn't know your sister helped you on it. I think that armor is so cool!" Looking at Eris, Aphrodite confided, "Last year, Ares even put a spell on it so it can talk."

"I wish I could learn magic," Eris said with a pout. "They don't teach it in the schools on Earth."

Ares didn't want to touch that subject with a ten-foot spear. "Well, now you've seen where I live," he told Eris quickly. Stashing his box of presents just inside the dorm hall for now, he firmly shut the door, blocking their view. Then he ushered the girls back down to the fourth floor, waiting for an opening to warn Aphrodite about Eris.

As if she'd guessed his intention, Eris talked the whole flight of stairs down, swinging her bag back and forth between her and Aphrodite. Whatever was inside it was definitely heavy, thought Ares, judging by the way it sagged at the bottom.

When the three of them arrived at the girls' dorm hall, Eris pushed Aphrodite in through the door, saying, "I'll be right there. I want to talk to my brother alone for a minute, okay? Haven't seen him in sooo long."

"Oh, okay," Aphrodite said. "Totally understandable. Well, my room's on the left when you're ready. Name's on the door.

"'Night, Ares," she called over her shoulder as she turned to go. She even blew him a kiss and sent him one of those beautiful smiles of hers that always managed to melt his heart. "Happy birthday, again!"

"G'night," Ares called back. He watched helplessly as the door slammed shut behind her.

Thonk! Eris set down her bag. For just a moment Ares glimpsed something made of gold metal at the top of the bag. Then whatever it was slid deeper inside. Was it the trophy Aphrodite has mentioned earlier? Only Eris had dismissed it as "nothing." So did that mean it wasn't a birthday gift for him? He was about to ask when his sister pinched his arm. *Hard.*

"Ow!" he yelled. Staring at her, he rubbed the place she'd pinched. "What did you do that for?" he asked, knowing it was a dumb question. Eris had never needed a reason to visit her torments on him before. So why would she need one now?

"Consider it a reminder," she informed him. Her eyes were gleaming again. "That if you dare to cross me, you'll regret it. I like it fine here at MOA, especially since it seems to be my only option right now. So I'm going to get Principal Zeus to let me go to school here."

"How? We're not twins, remember? So I don't really think that's an opt—*ow!*" Ares yelped. Eris had pinched him again. If only she were a guy. And bigger. Then he wouldn't let her get away with that kind of stuff!

She laughed. "Don't try to stop me from getting what I want. You'll be sorry if you do. There are sooo many embarrassing stories I could tell everyone at

MOA about you!" She eyed him evilly, tapping a finger on her chin. "Let's see. Like the time you wet the bed the night before battling your first beast. Or how you once almost poked your eye out with a toy spear."

"I was four years old!" he protested. He hunched his shoulder and looked around, hoping no one had overheard.

"Once a baby, always a baby," she taunted him, smirking. Her dark purple-blue eyes bored into his, still gleaming. "Those stories ought to impress Aphrodite and maybe all your guy friends, too, hmm?" She stretched on tiptoe and got into his face. "And maybe your enemies would be interested to know you sometimes carry your teddy bear into battle. Would you like that, Ares? Should I tell them all those things?"

Panic ripped through him. No, he did not want that! Aphrodite and his MOA friends looked up to him.

They thought him powerful, strong. A godboy without weaknesses. His sister could ruin his reputation here. Stop others from respecting him. A big part of winning competitions and battles was the fear and respect you inspired in your opponents. Who would respect him if they knew he *occasionally* took his good-luck teddy bear into a competition?

He broke away from her gaze to stare down at his sandaled feet. Only his sister had the ability to make him feel this powerless. "No, don't tell them," he said in a meek voice very unlike his normal one. A voice only she could cause him to use.

"Thought not," Eris said in triumph. "But don't worry, little brother. I won't breathe a word about your . . . *quirks* . . . as long as you keep out of my way." All at once she smiled sunnily. Picking up her bag again, she opened the door and stepped into the hall.

"Nite-nite, Ares. Oh, and like Aphrodite said—happy birthday!" she sang out. Then she let the door slam shut in his face.

Feeling doomed, Ares trudged back up to the guys' dorm and pulled open the door. After picking up his box of gifts, he started down the hall to his room. "Want some help?" he called out to Dionysus, who was painting purple racing stripes on one side of the half-built chariot. Apollo was helping out, hammering something on the chariot's other side.

Both godboys gave him a thumbs-up. "Yeah, sure!" said Dionysus. "You can help Apollo pound out the dents in the side panel."

Ares dropped his box of gifts along the wall and grabbed a hammer. Going to the other side of the chariot, he got on his knees and started whacking out dents. *Bam! Bam! Whack!* It felt good to get out his frustrations like this, and he was mostly quiet as his friends joked around.

Never before had he wished his guy friends talked about feelings and things like girls did. But right now he kind of wished they did. Aphrodite probably talked over all kinds of problems and shared tons of secrets with her friends. But he and the guys were more into *doing* stuff.

He slung his hammer. *Whack!* It wasn't like he could complain to his buds about Eris, though. He'd spent a lot of time at MOA these past years building up a reputation as a tough guy in order to be worthy of his title as godboy of war. If these guys guessed that his sister—to the untrained eye, a mere slip of a girl—could make him quake in his boots, he'd be a laughingstock.

When the work on the chariot eventually broke up for the night, he headed for his room, no closer to figuring out what to do about Eris. Just thinking about the way she'd outmaneuvered him tonight made him feel small and powerless all over again.

"Halt. Who goes there?" his suit of armor called out as he came even with the door of his room.

"What's it doing?" Dionysus called from across the hall, his hand on the doorknob to his and Apollo's room. Instead of letting Ares pass, the armor had raised its spear and pointed it at his chest. Or rather, at the box he was carrying against his chest.

"Godsamighty, it's me. Ares," he told it. "Don't you recognize me?"

The armor swayed back and forth, seeming confused. At last, it relented, lowering the spear to its side again. "Alack! For a moment I thought 'twas some small child."

Ares frowned. *Small child?* Maybe the spell he'd cast to make the armor recognize him was wearing off. Or had the box of presents blocked the suit of armor's view of him? Or maybe, since Eris had made him *feel* small, he'd actually seemed a child to the armor just then. What a horrifying thought.

Creeeak! The suit of armor bowed at the waist. "Pardon me, Sir Ares," it said. "You may pass."

"That was weird," he muttered to himself as he went inside his room. With a quick wave to Dionysus and Apollo, he kicked the door shut behind him and dropped his box of gifts to the floor. He heard something break inside. *Argh!*

After starting off so well, this birthday had turned out to be the worst one of his whole life! Thanks to his sister!

5

Teamwork

Aphrodite

I'M POOPED," ERIS ANNOUNCED THE MINUTE SHE entered Aphrodite's room. "Mind if I go straight to bed?"

Aphrodite had been flipping through a fashion scrollazine while waiting for Eris to join her, but she set it aside now and tried to hide her disappointment. "Oh. Okay. Sure." She'd been hoping to have a long chat with Eris before they settled down to sleep. To find out more about Ares. Eris probably had lots of cute stories about him she could share.

In the few minutes they had left, she gave it her best shot. "So I'm dying to know what Ares was like when you guys were growing up. I bet he was adorable!"

Eris shrugged, then yawned. "Oh, you know."

No, she didn't know. And she wanted to! Ares rarely talked about his childhood or feelings. This was her chance to find out more about him. And she'd also hoped she might get to see the trophy again or learn something that might help her win tomorrow's Two Truths and a Lie game. Not that she would ever cheat, of course.

"You can sleep there," Aphrodite said, gesturing toward her spare bed. Like her own bed just opposite, it was covered with a plush red velvet comforter stitched with a pattern of little white hearts.

Eris reached out to squeeze one of the puffy, heart-shaped pillows at the head of the bed, leaving it bunched and lumpy-looking. Aphrodite's fingers twitched with the desire to pat it back into shape, but she resisted the urge and watched Eris set the bag with its precious trophy under the bed.

"I'll need to borrow a nightgown," Eris said.

"Oh, of course," Aphrodite said quickly. She grabbed a cute one from her closet and held it out.

Eris frowned at it. "Pink ruffles? Don't you have anything nicer?"

"That's my best one," said Aphrodite, taken aback. Really, Ares's sister could learn a few manners! Saying so wouldn't help her make friends with the girl, however, so she kept silent. She was determined to befriend Eris. After all, she was Ares's sister. And Aphrodite had often longed for family of her own. Maybe Eris could become the sister she'd never had. Though no matter what, she'd still have her GGBFFs, of course.

Eris squinched up her nose and took the nightgown, holding it with just the tips of her fingers as if she didn't really want to touch it. "Guess this will have to do," she said with a sigh. After changing into it, she flopped onto Aphrodite's spare bed, pulled the comforter up to her chin, and went straight to sleep.

Aphrodite was about to climb into bed herself a few minutes later when her eyes fell on the trophy bag. It was sticking out a bit from under Eris's bed. An urge pulled at her to sneak the golden apple trophy out of it. Just for a minute. Only to admire it again. She went closer and bent, reaching.

Ermmm. Eris turned over in her sleep, snuffling a little.

Aphrodite leaped back. *Ye gods!* How embarrassing if she'd gotten caught snooping in another girl's schoolbag! Wondering what in the world had gotten into her, she made herself resist further temptation.

Besides, she was tired too. Planning Ares's birthday party had been a lot of work. She smiled as she snuggled into bed. He'd enjoyed it, though, which had made all her efforts worth it.

"I borrowed something to wear," Eris announced the minute Aphrodite woke the next morning. The girl was already dressed—in Aphrodite's newest pink chiton, no less. She hadn't even had a chance to wear it herself yet!

"Figured you wouldn't mind," Eris explained as Aphrodite sat up. "Oh, I've decided I like pink after all."

"Looks nice on you," said Aphrodite. In truth, her chiton looked a little too big on the petite girl, but she decided not to say so. She was determined to be a good host.

Eris was sitting in the desk chair, Aphrodite's magic makeup brush hovering above her head. When she raised her face to it, it swooped in to add a touch of blush to her cheeks. She stretched her fingers out before her. Immediately, another smaller magic brush dipped its bristles into a bottle of Tropical Sunset Pink polish and began painting it back and forth over Eris's nails. Aphrodite had bought that polish at the Immortal Marketplace only last week.

Hey, help yourself, why don't you? Aphrodite felt like saying. But then she decided it was kind of cool in a way. Almost like they were sisters. Because sisters shared clothes and makeup, right? That's what she'd heard, anyway. Just like she sometimes shared with her friends. But her friends usually asked first. Maybe sisters didn't, though. She'd have to ask Medusa sometime.

"So what are your plans?" she asked Eris, padding

104

over to her closet. "What do you want to do while every-one's in classes? I could show you where the library is and you could hang out there till lunch." She opened her closet to pull out a fresh chiton to wear and then gasped. A heap of chitons lay balled up at the bottom!

Hearing her, Eris looked over. "Oh, yeah, I tried those on before finding one cute enough to actually wear."

A prickle of irritation swept over Aphrodite. Didn't this girl have any manners at all? As she shook out the wrinkles in the discarded chitons and hung them up again, Eris blew on her nails to dry them.

"Don't worry about me. I've got plans," Eris informed her. Her eyes glinted in the morning light filtering in through the window. "Wish me luck."

"Luck?" said Aphrodite as she slipped a fresh chiton over her head. "What for?"

"I'm going to the office to talk Zeus into letting me

move here and go to MOA," Eris said in a determined voice.

It was obvious how much Ares's sister wanted to attend the Academy. It was a good reminder to Aphrodite of how lucky she was to be enrolled here herself. If she'd never been admitted to MOA, she'd never have met Athena, Artemis, and Persephone. Or Ares! "Well, good luck. I'm sure it would be fun for you and Ares if that worked out. And speaking of Ares . . ." she said, returning to the topic of the night before, "what was he like when you guys were growing up?"

"Dorky, like most brothers," Eris said flatly. Which was not at all helpful or interesting. Not only that, Aphrodite doubted it was true. Ares was many things. But he could never be a dork.

Her gaze fell on the spare bed. Eris's bag was lying on top of the rumpled coverlet. The bag with the trophy. She could hardly believe she'd almost snooped in it last night! Though the trophy didn't seem quite as enticing now as it had then for some reason, she still wanted it. Wanted to hold it again. Possess it. She followed Eris to the door and gestured toward the bag she held. "Could I maybe see—"

But Eris interrupted. "I'm going to grab a bite to eat in the cafeteria before I pin down . . . um . . . *have a chat* with Principal Zeus. See you!" she called back over her shoulder. Then she headed off down the hall, leaving the bed unmade and the makeup she'd borrowed spread out across Aphrodite's desk.

Well, so much for getting another look at that cool trophy, Aphrodite thought as she began straightening the spare bed. Or pumping Eris for info about Ares's childhood. Or getting any inside tips about the Two Truths and a Lie game.

Of its own accord, her magic rouge brush sailed back into its box, when she went over to clean up the makeup mess Eris had left behind. She wasn't sure how much success Ares's sister would have with Principal Zeus. He'd been clear last night that she would have to leave today after dinner. Even Ares seemed unsure about having her here.

Since Aphrodite didn't have any family at all, she totally got why Eris wanted to enroll at MOA. If she had a brother going here—especially a cool one like Ares—she'd want to be with him, too. Still, although Aphrodite admired Eris's spunk, it seemed unlikely her chat with Zeus was going to work. He was pretty picky about who he allowed to go to school here and had even been known to kick students out on a whim. Besides that, he could be really hardheaded and difficult to convince about things that weren't his idea!

. . .

"What did you and Eris talk about last night after the party ended? The game? The trophy?" Athena asked Aphrodite at lunch. Artemis and Persephone raised their eyebrows at her questions. Morning classes had flown by, and now all four friends were at their usual table in the cafeteria.

Why did Athena sound so anxious? Aphrodite wondered. Was it just curiosity about Eris? Or something to do with that trophy? Her own desire to win it spiked up a notch as she realized Athena still wanted it too. She didn't really like feeling competitive with one of her very best friends like this, though.

She set down the carton of nectar she'd been sipping. "I didn't actually get a chance to talk to her much. She went to sleep as soon as her head hit the pillow. And she was up and out of my room this morning before I was even dressed."

Athena's shoulders seemed to relax a little at this news.

"So she stayed the night with you?" Persephone asked Aphrodite, her green eyes blinking. "I thought she was only here for the party."

"After you left, Principal Zeus told her she could stay on till after dinner today," Artemis informed her.

"Long enough to finish last night's game," added Athena. She and Aphrodite glanced at each other warily, then both of them looked away.

"Wonder where she is now?" Artemis shifted the bow and quiver of arrows strung over her back and glanced around the room.

"ATTENTION, STUDENTS!" a voice boomed out just then. Everyone in the cafeteria jumped at the sudden command.

"Ah! Question answered," Artemis murmured, taking a bite of her nectarburger.

All eyes turned toward Principal Zeus as he strode to the middle of the cafeteria. Eris was at his side, her apple trophy bag clutched tightly to her chest.

"Somebody looks happy," Persephone murmured.

She was right. Eris was beaming brighter than Helios the sun god's golden chariot. Did that mean what Aphrodite thought it meant? Could Eris have won Zeus over so quickly?

Zeus's gold bracelets flashed as he crossed his muscular arms over his massive chest and planted his feet wide. "Last night I began going over your semester-end grades," he called out to students in a thunderous voice. "And I finished the job this morning." He frowned, and his bushy red eyebrows jammed together. "Except for a few notable exceptions, your results were less than stellar. In fact, they were dismal." His piercing blue eyes swept the crowd as he paused to let this disastrous news sink in.

No one dared breathe a word as he finally went on. "I have to say, I'm SERIOUSLY disappointed in you all. Mortals look up to us. This Academy has STANDARDS to uphold. Standards of the absolute highest, and—"

As he continued to drone on about MOA's standards and the importance of meeting them, Aphrodite peeked over at Athena. Her shoulders were slumped, and she was looking really upset. Almost as if she believed herself personally responsible for everyone's awful grades. For Athena, slacking off would mean getting a mere A on a paper or test instead of her usual A plus!

Persephone nudged Athena. "Not your fault," she whispered with a sympathetic smile. Aphrodite nodded, but Athena was looking the other way and didn't notice her show of support.

Lightening up a little now, Zeus was saying, "Though hugely disappointed at your results, I've decided to give you all additional time to bring those grades up before taking any sterner measures." Out of the corner of her eye, Aphrodite saw him shoot Eris a sidelong glance. "And I have a plan to help assure your success. A 'friendly competition' between two teams to see who can earn the best grades by the end of the next two weeks!"

Dead silence filled the cafeteria for a few seconds. Then Eris piped up. "It'll make learning more *fun*. Promise!"

Hmm, thought Aphrodite. She'd bet her best pink chiton (the one that Eris happened to be wearing), that Zeus's success plan had come from Ares's sister! When he heard an idea he liked, it could be pretty easy to convince him that he'd thought it up in the first place. Had Eris figured that out?

"As team leaders, I've chosen two Hero-ology students who recently succeeded in leading the great hero Odysseus safely home to his family," Zeus continued.

Electric sparks shot from the ends of his fingers as his arm swung out, causing the students nearest him to duck. He pointed toward Aphrodite and her friends' table.

"One team will be headed by Theeny, my most favorite daughter in the whole wide universe. And the other team by Aphrodite!" Zeus boomed.

Aphrodite sat bolt upright, startled to hear him name her as the second team leader. *Athena* had been mainly responsible for guiding Odysseus home. All Aphrodite had done was work at keeping his wife, Penelope, safe from suitors until he could get back to Ithaca. Because, thinking Odysseus was dead, the suitors had wanted to marry Penelope and take over Odysseus's estate.

Hmm. Eris was grinning from ear to ear now. Aphrodite had a funny feeling that the choice of team leaders had been her idea as well! But why?

114

"There will be prizes galore for the team that wins," Zeus promised. "As for the losing team, they will have to act as servants to the winning team for one entire day!"

As the students whooped their approval of the competition prizes, Eris held her black bag high. "And a special prize will go to the winning team *leader*!" she called out.

She must mean the trophy, Aphrodite thought. Picturing the lovely golden apple at its top, a small spark of yearning flamed brightly inside her and she wished she could see it and hold it right now. She saw a similar spark in Athena's eyes.

As for Eris, she seemed oblivious that Zeus had begun scowling at her. She really should be more careful about making such comments, thought Aphrodite. He didn't like to be upstaged. Catching her eye just then, the girl winked at her. Then she lowered the bag to her side.

Clank! Athena had finished her ambrosia salad and had begun to stack her dishes on her tray with a little more force than necessary. "What did that mean?" she demanded suspiciously. "That wink."

Aphrodite spread her hands, feeling defensive. "I don't know. She told me she wants to go to MOA. Maybe she thinks this competition is her ticket in."

Persephone tilted her chin in thought. "I wonder if this new contest idea of Zeus's could actually be *her* idea."

Aphrodite nodded. "I was thinking the same thing."

"Probably found out that Zeus was upset about semester grades and used that information to her advantage," said Artemis, tossing bits of her nectar-burger under the table to her dogs.

Athena's expression softened, and she smiled fondly. "My dad does love a good competition."

"So are you guys going to pick teams, or what?" Persephone asked.

"No clue," said Aphrodite. And she was a little worried that everyone would want to be on Athena's team, given how brainy she was.

But then Zeus announced that the two teams had already been decided. "Ms. Hydra has randomly assigned names to two lists," he announced. After producing two small scrolls tied with ribbons from the pocket of his tunic, he called Athena and Aphrodite up beside him and presented one listscroll to each of them.

Aphrodite caught Ares's eye in the crowd. For some reason, he looked worried. Did he think her team wouldn't have a chance of beating Athena's? Her already fragile confidence wavered.

Zeus smiled at Athena and Aphrodite, his white teeth gleaming. "I'm counting on you to do your very best to inspire your teams," he told them. "Eris has some good ideas for the contest, and since she's currently on semester break, she has offered to stay on at MOA to help. She'll be keeping score for your teams during the next two weeks and reporting to me how things are going."

Turning back to the gathered students, he clapped his big hands together. "That's it, then. Athena and Aphrodite will read the team assignments!" With a curt nod, he turned abruptly and strode from the cafeteria.

"So no more Two Truths and a Lie game?" Athena asked Eris.

"Forget that. This competition will be way more fun. Isn't it cool that I talked Zeus into naming you team leaders?" Eris told them as they untied their scrolls. "Just think, one of you will definitely win this!" She patted her trophy bag meaingfully.

Aphrodite shrugged, feeling her interest in the

trophy sag. Being a team leader was going to be a big responsibility. Athena didn't look all that thrilled either.

Seeming a little alarmed at their lack of enthusiasm, Eris pulled the trophy from her bag and pushed it into Athena's hand, causing her to drop her team list.

Hardly realizing what she was doing, Aphrodite quickly stuffed her own list into the pocket of her chiton. She couldn't resist reaching toward Athena to run her hand over the brightly polished golden apple at its top. Just touching the trophy again strengthened her competitive spirit. Suddenly, she felt more determined than ever to win it!

She looked at Athena and saw the same desire to win surge into her eyes. *Uh-oh.*

"This is going to be awesome," Eris enthused as she slipped the trophy back into its bag. "Of course, your smarts will probably give your team the edge over

Aphrodite's," she said to Athena. "Your grades alone would raise any team's overall score."

"Think so?" Athena was beaming. "Thanks!"

Aphrodite felt a stab of jealousy. Her grades had always been pretty good, but even if she studied all day and all night she'd never achieve the kind of perfect grades her brainy friend Athena got. No one at MOA could.

Nervously, she fingered the double-G-shaped charm that hung from the gold necklace that she and all three of her besties wore. The necklaces were a symbol of their friendship, only right now that friendship was feeling a little strained.

"On the other hand," Eris said, turning toward Aphrodite, "it'll take more than a single team captain's over-the-top grades to win this competition. I bet all of the boys, not just my brother, will study superhard if they think it'll impress you. And I've heard that the girls look to you to set fashion trends, so if studying becomes mega-fashionable, well . . . I think you can see what I'm saying."

Aphrodite smiled, her confidence restored. Eris was right. With a bit of motivation, there was every reason to hope that her team could best Athena's. Out of the corner of her eye, she glimpsed Athena anxiously biting her lip. *Ha!* Seemed like the sandal was on the other foot now!

Eris quickly explained the rules she and Zeus had come up with to both girls. "Students on each team will earn points for their team every day based on grades made on quizzes, tests, projects, and reports. A's earn fifteen points. B's earn ten points. C's, five. But D's and F's earn zilch. Teachers will report test grades each day, and it's my job to add them up. Got it?"

Athena and Aphrodite nodded together.

"Hey! Who wants to hear the team lists?" Eris called out to the cafeteria.

Everyone cheered and clapped enthusiastically. With just minutes left in the lunch period, the two goddessgirls pulled out the lists Zeus had given them. A hush fell over the students as the girls quickly unrolled and scanned their listscrolls.

Aphrodite frowned when she saw that Ares was not on her list. *Drat.* That meant her crush would be competing on the opposing team. Then she discovered that Heracles *was* on her team. Since he was Athena's crush, that seemed to even things up a little. Their two best buds were split up too, she noticed. Artemis was on Aphrodite's team, but Persephone wasn't. For a randomly designed list, it actually seemed pretty fair.

"I'll need a place to stay. So I thought I'd trade off with you both," Eris told Athena and Aphrodite quickly. "One night in one room and the next in the other. Back and forth, you know?"

"Athena has a roommate. You can stay with me, though," said Aphrodite. It might give her an edge.

"No! Pandora likes dogs and snakes. She won't mind staying with Artemis or Medusa every other night," Athena insisted.

Aphrodite doubted Pandora would appreciate being booted out of her room every other night for two weeks, but whatever!

"Cool!" said Eris. Then, stepping between the two girls, she put an arm around each of their shoulders. She looked out over the cafeteria crowd. "Okay," she shouted. "Let's read out the teams lists and get this competition started!"

6

Obsessed

Ares

A LITTLE OVER A WEEK LATER, ARES WAS AT HIS
locker after school when he overheard Aphrodite speaking in a sharp tone. He looked over to see she'd cornered
Poseidon, who was a member of her team in the grades
competition, at his locker.

"You made a C on your Science-ology quiz?" she
exclaimed, shaking the papyrus quiz under Poseidon's

nose. "I expected better from you. *Much* better."

"Well, I am the godboy of the C's," Poseidon joked. "Get it? Seas as in oceans and C's as in the letter *C*?"

The old Aphrodite would have laughed, even if it was kind of a lame joke. But not the new *team leader* Aphrodite.

"Your quiz grade is going to drag our team down," she scolded him. "And we've only got till Friday—*four days*—to win this thing. You need to shape up and study harder."

Looking apologetic, Poseidon ducked his head. "Okay," he mumbled. "I'll try."

"You'd better," she told him. "There's a lot at stake here, buster."

Ares shook his head in disbelief. Both Aphrodite and Athena were taking this competition way too seriously. Over the past week, point totals had seesawed back and forth with Aphrodite's team ahead one day and Athena's the next. Team members had stayed friendly toward one another during the first few days. There had even been a lot of joking about what kind of servant work each student would get another to do if their team lost.

Medusa swore to get her sisters to clean her room. Iris, who had recently been named the goddessgirl of rainbows, planned to have students polish the rainbows she created, to travel on as slides for delivering messages. And Poseidon was going to get students to clean the statues in the outdoor fountains he'd designed around the school.

However, as the second week had begun and the end of the contest approached, the atmosphere at MOA had grown decidedly tense.

As soon as Poseidon took off, Ares went over to Aphrodite. "Don't you think you were kind of rough on him?" he asked, falling into step with her as she took off down the hall. "Anyone would think that *you* are the god of war instead of me. You're making this whole grades contest into a battle!"

"I'm a *goddess*, not a god," Aphrodite said testily. "And this *is* a battle. One I intend to win, by the way." She narrowed her eyes at him. "No thanks to you!"

Ouch, thought Ares. Guess she'd found out about that A he'd made on this morning's Science-ology quiz. Which had increased the point totals for *Athena's* team, of course. Ever since this competition had started, he'd felt torn. He was competitive himself and wanted to be a good team player and perform well for himself. And for his team and the school. But whenever he turned in a good grade on a test or a report, Aphrodite made him feel like a traitor.

Spotting Heracles, who was also on her team, Aphrodite sped off down the hall. "Hey, Heracles! What's this about a B minus in Literature-ology?"

Heracles was no fool. He zoomed out the front door of the Academy before she could nab him.

Ares joined Aphrodite outside on MOA's front steps. She was standing with her hands on her hips, watching Heracles disappear toward the sports fields, a huge frown on her face. Now was probably not the best time to mention his sister's earlier advice against frowning, he figured.

"You tell your lion-caped buddy that he'd better shape up or else," she instructed Ares, all in a huff.

"Yes, sir!" he said, saluting her.

"Not funny," she said, glaring at him. "Have you seen Pandora? Oh, there she is." Seeing the blue-and-gold-haired girl in the courtyard, she zoomed after her, the next victim on her team.

She hadn't even noticed that Ares was wearing the new Fly like the Wind sandals she'd given him for his birthday. For now, the sandals' laces were tied loosely around the wings to keep them still so he could walk at a normal speed. He'd free the wings once he hit the sports fields for track practice. It was time to start seriously training for these upcoming war games.

After taking the granite steps downward, he crossed the courtyard and was halfway to the sports fields when he heard a sound.

"Psst!" It was Heracles. He was hiding behind a fountain alongside the path. "Where's Aphrodite? Is the coast clear?"

Ares couldn't help laughing. "Are you kidding me? You're actually scared of the goddess of love?" Heracles was taller and stronger than *him,* even though both boys were equally muscular and Heracles was a mortal.

Heracles straightened his lion cape and stepped onto the path, looking a little embarrassed. "Didn't you hear her back there? Your crush can be scary, god-dude." He gave a mock-shiver.

"Yeah, yours too," said Ares. "I've been making A's partly just to avoid Athena's wrath."

"This whole grades competition thing is getting worse and worse," Heracles complained as the two of them continued on to the sports fields. "It's starting to stink more than cow poop in King Augeas's stables!"

Ares grinned. "That bad, huh?" Cleaning up the king's enormous stables had been one of twelve labors Heracles had had to perform before gaining a perma-nent place at MOA. Though Ares hadn't been there to help, he could imagine how those stables must have reeked. *P-U!*

"Don't blame Aphrodite," said Ares. "Eris has been dodging me all week, so I haven't been able to ask her, but I'm guessing that this whole grades contest was her idea."

"Yeah? Hey, what's up with that apple trophy of hers, anyway?" Heracles asked.

"Trophy?" Ares repeated. His mind clicked on the gold metal item he'd seen at the top of Eris's black bag outside the girls' dorm the night of his birthday party.

"God-dude, haven't you heard about it?" Heracles asked. "Athena's, like, *obsessed* with winning it. It's like that thing's put her under some kind of enchantment."

"Enchantment?" mused Ares. "Hmm." Could an enchanted trophy be affecting Aphrodite's behavior too? "I wonder if you could be—*oomph!*" He broke off, stumbling a few steps forward as someone shoved him from behind.

Ares whirled around to face off with . . . his roommate? Atlas, who was also MOA's bulky champion weightlifter, was glaring at him. "What was that for?" Ares asked him in surprise.

Atlas hooked a thumb toward Heracles. "Why are

you talking to the enemy?" he growled. "It's bad enough that you're still hanging out with his team captain."

"*Enemy? Heracles?* So suddenly we can't hang out just because he's on the opposite team in this dumb grades contest?" Ares said in disbelief. Even though Atlas had some Titan parentage and Olympians weren't usually pals with Titans, all three boys had always been buds!

"Some friend you are, Heracles," Atlas retorted. "Don't think I've forgotten how you tricked me into holding up the sky while you stole those magic apples." He looked ready to fight! The three boys squared off, their muscles stiff, prepared for trouble.

"The ones from the Garden of the Hesperides? That happened forever ago!" Heracles protested. "Besides, getting those apples was one of the labors I had to do in order to stay at MOA. And I sent Ares and Poseidon back to get you later, didn't I?"

"Yeah, he did," Ares put in.

But Atlas only snorted, unimpressed. "Because Athena told you to," he countered, glaring at Heracles. "At least that's the way I heard it."

"Who told you that? *Athena?*" Heracles demanded. Now he sounded tense, too, and the two boys began circling each other in a fighting stance.

"Wait!" Ares ordered. Leaping between them, he held his arms straight out from his sides to keep them apart. Sounded like Heracles' friendship with Athena had taken a hit recently, just like his own friendship with Aphrodite had. Things with her been going pretty well before this competition started. But by now Aphrodite had become downright *snippy* with him.

"In case you forgot, we didn't *choose* which teams to be on; we were *assigned* to them," Ares told the guys. Although, knowing his sister, it wouldn't surprise him if she had a hand in helping Ms. Hydra make the "random" assignments so they best pitted friend against friend. "Godsamighty! How come everyone else but me is fighting these days when *I'm* the godboy of war?"

Atlas ignored him and started jogging off backward. On the way, he picked up a statue along the side of the path and started pumping it up and down overhead with one arm. Since he was the school's champion weightlifter, he was always grabbing random stuff to pump like that.

"You just wait," he told Heracles. "When this contest ends on Friday, our team is going to *crush* yours. Then I'll make you my servant for a day, like Principal Zeus promised. And I'll find something for you to do that's even harder than holding up the sky! Like maybe holding up your big fat head!" With that final threat hanging in the air, he tossed the statue back to stand at one side of the path and turned to jog off toward the gymnasium.

"I hope your workout improves your personality!" Heracles yelled after him. When one of the discus throwers in a nearby section of field called to Heracles just then, he told Ares bye and loped off in that direction.

Ye gods! This whole grades contest was totally out of control! thought Ares as he headed for the track. After a few warm-up stretches, he freed the wings on his new sandals and began flying laps around the obstacle course, still thinking about what had happened as he traveled.

Skimming a few inches above the ground, he ducked under bars, spun around as he leaped over small hills he encountered, and banked around sharp curves. The course was magical, so it changed when you least expected it and was always different each time you flew it. The athletic Temple Games weren't taking place for another month and a half, but he needed that time to get in shape for them. He had just finished his third lap when he suddenly remembered Heracles' remark about Eris's trophy.

Could it really be enchanted? Or maybe her power to create discord had simply rubbed off on it, making Athena and Aphrodite ultracompetitive all of a sudden? He stopped to do chin-ups on a bar beside the track. Up. Down. Up. Down. Up. Hey! He did a double take when he saw his sister skimming across the courtyard in a pair of winged sandals she must have borrowed from the communal basket beside MOA's front doors.

At last! It was high time for a little talk, he decided grimly. Ares dropped from the bars, then whisked across the sports fields. Training could wait.

"Where are you headed?" he asked when he finally caught up with his sister.

Eris stopped dead, whipping around so fast, she fell over. She did not look pleased to see him.

He glanced down the path in the direction she'd been traveling, which went to Earth. "Going home for a visit?"

"Maybe. So?" she said guardedly. She ignored the helping hand he held out and pushed to her feet on her own, apple trophy bag and all.

"So nothing," Ares said. His eyes went to her lumpy bag, and he reached out for it. "Hey, let me see that trophy a second."

Her eyes went wide, and she wrapped both arms around the bag. "Why?" she asked, sounding nervous.

Ares lunged for the bag, but she swung it away from him just in time and skimmed off. He gave chase, calling, "I'll go to Principal Zeus about this if I have to!"

Eris screeched to a halt, looking trapped. He was usually the one backing down from *her*, but now she caved instead for once. "Okay," she said reluctantly. "You can have one quick look." She started to slide the trophy from the bag.

Ares swung out an arm. "Gotcha!" he crowed, whipping the trophy from the bag. He zoomed off with it now, winged sandals flying. His new ones were far faster than her borrowed ones, and he easily outpaced her.

"Give that back!" Eris protested behind him, frantically trying to catch up.

But Ares ignored her. As he flew on, he turned the trophy this way and that in his hands. He'd halfway expected to feel an uncontrollable urge to possess it. However, when he didn't, he slowed, stopping.

Eris caught up to him and snatched at her trophy. Still, he held her off. She was acting really anxious now, studying his face.

"Worried I'll go gaga over it, like Aphrodite and

Athena?" he asked. "And what does this inscription mean—*For the Fairest*?"

"Nothing. I don't know what you're talking about. If Aphrodite and Athena are acting different, chalk it up to the competitive instinct to win, I guess," Eris replied smoothly. "You should know all about that, war boy!"

Ha! "I don't believe you. What's so special about this thing? It's not having any effect on me. Seems like a standard-issue trophy. Is it enchanted?" he demanded, finally handing it back to her. Being a good athlete, he had a whole roomful of trophies, many much nicer than her apple one.

"How could it be? You just said it felt like a plain ol' trophy to you." A look of pleased relief flashed across Eris's face and then it was gone. Maybe he'd only imagined it, he decided, since now she was smirking. "So I hope you're satisfied," she said, rebagging the trophy.

They slowly circled each other, their winged sandals hovering a few inches above the forest path as they stared each other down. "Something's different," Ares said at last. "You're bigger. Taller. More powerful. You're enjoying stirring up trouble here, aren't you?" He knew from experience that the confidence she got from making trouble increased her stature and strength. *Literally.*

"Yeah, MOA agrees with me," she said unapologetically. "Some of the kids are kind of standoffish, though, like I make them nervous or something."

He eyed her. If word had gotten around about his sister being the goddess of strife and discord—which was likely with Pheme's nose for gossip—then he could well imagine that some kids might be "standoffish" around her.

"But Aphrodite—I mean, I can see why you like her," Eris went on. "She's been so nice, letting me borrow her chitons to wear and everything." She twirled in a quick circle to show off the one she had on now.

No surprise that he hadn't recognized the chiton she had on as one of Aphrodite's. He paid about as much attention to clothes as his godboy friends did. Which was to say, not much. She must've sensed that he was about to question her further about the trophy because she burst into speech before he could break in.

"Zeus is really happy with the results my contest is getting so far," she boasted in a rush. "Grades are up across the board. He says teachers report that students have been working much harder in class." She paused, and that all-too-familiar gleam came into her eyes.

Ares's gaze narrowed. "What I want to know is, what's in this for you?"

"A spot at MOA, of course! Zeus is bound to invite me to enroll once I've proven my value around here. I'll get him to change that dumb no-siblings-who-aren't-twins-or-triplets rule."

Suddenly Eris whisked closer and darted a hand toward him. He flinched, expecting to be punched or pinched. Instead, much to his surprise, she *hugged* him!

"Wha-what was that for?" he asked, stumbling back from her.

She rolled her eyes. "A thank-you for not ratting me out about being expelled from my last school. And anyway, since when does a big sister *need* a reason to give her little brother a hug?"

Ares gaped at her. She'd never needed a reason to pinch or haul off and slug him, either! But she'd done that plenty.

"See you!" With a bright smile and a little wave, Eris and her bag were off!

Ares watched her go, feeling totally confused. Once,

long ago, his parents had told him that it was his job to protect Eris since she was his sister. She'd never seemed in need of protection to him, though. If anything, he'd been the one needing protection. From *her*!

But was it possible his sister was turning over a new leaf? he wondered as he skimmed back to the Academy. If given the chance to enroll at MOA, could she change for the better? Doubtful. She was just riding high on success. It was making her act halfway nice for once.

When he reached MOA, he looped the laces on his Fly like the Wind sandals around the wings at his heels to still them. Then he pushed through the bronze doors and started down the hall to his next class.

Sure, students' grades had gone up as a result of the competition, but at what cost? Heracles and Atlas were barely speaking. Roommates and friends were at one another's throats. The tension between the competing teams was tight as a wire, and soon that wire was going to snap. Maybe it already had, he realized as he rounded a corner and ran smack into a shouting match between two of his best friends. Ares joined the crowd of students who had gathered around them to watch.

"It's your fault I messed up on that monster identification test in Beast-ology today!" Poseidon yelled at Apollo. The godboy of the sea (or lately, *C's*) pointed his trident at Apollo in a menacing way. Poseidon was on Aphrodite's team, while Apollo was on Athena's, same as Ares.

"You accusing me of something?" Apollo shot back. "What's the matter? Scared that big, bad Aphrodite's going to lecture you?"

Instantly taking Poseidon's side, the other students on Aphrodite's team roared indignantly, while the students on Athena's team booed.

"You know you tricked me!" Poseidon yelled at Apollo. "I thought you were trying to help when you let me borrow your notes to study from last night, but you'd changed them all around so they were wrong. Turns out the kobaloi are sprites, not *spiders*, and they're fond of *tricking* mortals, not *tickling* them!"

Several students who were on the same team as Apollo laughed. Apollo just smirked and said, "Maybe you just couldn't read my handwriting."

"Ha!" yelled Poseidon. "You wanted me to screw up so your team could earn more points!" With that, he sprayed Apollo with water from the drippy three-pronged end of his trident, drenching the godboy from head to toe. Then he took off running.

Now Poseidon's supporters laughed. "Serves you right!" one of them jeered at Apollo.

"Godsamighty!" Apollo yelled as a puddle formed at

his feet. "I'll get you for this if it's the last thing I—" He started to run after Poseidon, but just then the lyrebell pinged a warning that the next period was about to start.

As everyone moved on to their classes, Ares went up to Apollo. "Sorry about that, buddy—" he began.

Apollo cut him off. "Yeah, I bet you are." Spinning on one heel, he stalked off to his next class, leaving Ares openmouthed in the middle of the hallway.

"Hey! What did I do? I'm on your team, remember?" he called after Apollo. This stupid grades contest! He couldn't wait till it was over.

He wanted his sister to be happy, but this was just a small taste of how *un*happy things were going get for everyone if she got her way and was allowed to become a permanent MOA student. She had to go!

7

Liars and Cheats

Aphrodite

"OKAY, TEAM!" APHRODITE SHOUTED. IT WAS
after school on Wednesday, and she stood at the top of the
granite steps that led from the Academy's big bronze front
doors down to the marble courtyard. Half the student
body—her team in the grades competition—had gathered
on the steps below her with some members spilling out
into the courtyard. She'd called them here for a pep talk.

Aphrodite raised her pink megaphone to her mouth. "Are you ready to win this thing!" she yelled in the enthusiastic voice she used for Cheer Squad.

"Ready!" her team yelled back.

"That's the spirit!" she responded. Truth, though, Eris had just informed her that her team was trailing Athena's by several points. That wasn't necessarily cause for alarm, as the lead had seesawed back and forth throughout the contest. But today was Wednesday. There were only three more days counting today until the contest was over!

"Now, what will we all be doing tonight?" she shouted through her megaphone.

"Studying!" her team yelled back.

"That's right!" Aphrodite encouraged. Then she led them in a cheer she'd composed especially for this rally:

"Come on, team—we can do it!

We're the best—and we can prove it!

We will burn that midnight oil,

And with all our mighty toil,

The other team's hopes, we will spoil!

Get on your feet, and let us hear it!

(Stomp! Stomp! Stomp-stomp-stomp!)

Hands together, let's all cheer it!

(Clap! Clap! Clap-clap-clap!)

Go, study, win! Go, study, WINNN!"

At the end of the cheer, her team erupted in enthusiastic yells and applause. Some of the girls even did air
splits, while the guys punched fists in the air. Then, with
renewed energy and determination, they started back
inside the Academy to go up to their rooms or to the
library to study. Too bad students couldn't earn points

for team spirit, Aphrodite thought. Her team would win hands down. Or rather, hands waving up in the air!

Unfortunately, two godboys named Makhai and Kydoimos, were hanging out on a bench just inside the Academy's front doors when Aphrodite's team broke up and started inside. They were on Athena's team, like Ares, who got along with them for some strange reason.

As she followed the last of her team inside, the two boys jumped up. Makhai pulled a quizscroll from his pocket and waved it in front of her face. There was an A plus grade on it. She'd heard some complaints about these bullies lately. A few of her team members suspected that they were cheating to better their grades.

"Read it and weep!" the squinty-eyed Makhai told her.

Kydoimos waved his quizscroll, too, also graded A plus. "Your team is toast!" he crowed.

"Get away from her, you . . . you *cheaters*!" shouted a

centaur on Aphrodite's team. Like many of the boys at MOA, this centaur—half boy and half horse—had long had a crush on her, she knew. Now he pawed at the marble floor with one of his front hooves and lowered his head like he was getting ready to charge the two boys.

"Cool it, Four Legs!" said Makhai. He sounded cocky, but he took a step back from her would-be champion nonetheless. "You're just jealous."

Then he spoke louder to the dozen members of Aphrodite's team who hadn't yet disappeared down the hall to the library or started upstairs to their rooms. "Instead of wasting your time with cheers, maybe Aphrodite should have organized you guys into study groups like Athena did with *our* team. Then you might actually have had a chance at winning this Friday. But no, you'll all wind up servants instead. Hahaha!" The two boys cracked up.

An angry murmur ran through Aphrodite's team.

She aimed her megaphone toward the two bullies as she spoke to her team beyond them. "I appreciate the support and loyalty," she called out. "But just ignore these guys. They know we'll win!"

"Ow! Watch it with that thing." Makhai and Kydoimos covered their ears and cringed away from her mega-loud voice.

"Oops! Sorry," she said sweetly, though she wasn't. She'd spoken with confidence to her team. However she *was* a little worried, actually. Because there just might be some truth in what Makhai had said. Athena's study groups must really be effective if this pair had managed to ace that quiz.

As if they had suddenly realized how outnumbered they were, the two boys ducked past Aphrodite and pushed outside through the front doors. "Bye, losers!" Kydoimos yelled back over his shoulder.

Poseidon and a couple of other godboys on her team made a lunge to follow. "Let's get 'em!"

Aphrodite threw her arms wide across the open doorway. "Stop!" she yelled, appalled. "No fighting!" She wanted her team to win, but despite what she'd said to Ares by the lockers the day before, she did *not* want a battle on her hands. After all, she was the goddessgirl of love! Sure, she and Athena had kind of been avoiding each other lately, but at least they'd remained civil whenever they did meet. And though Athena wasn't around right now, Aphrodite knew she'd have been just as upset by Makhai's and Kydoimos's behavior, too.

Luckily, Aphrodite's team obeyed her. To be sure none of them changed their minds and decided to go after Makhai and Kydoimos after all, however, she kept an eye on her remaining team members as they started up the stairs.

She was about to go up herself when Ares came in behind her through the still-open front doors. He was wearing his new Fly like the Wind winged sandals that she'd bought for his birthday, so she assumed he'd been out on the obstacle course.

"Hey," he said. "How's it going?"

"Don't you know?" she said stiffly. "Your team's ahead with only Thursday and Friday to go." Though she knew she shouldn't expect him to do poorly in his classes on purpose, she was kind of miffed at him for the high grades he'd been getting lately. Grades that boosted Athena's team scores, of course.

He rubbed the back of his neck, looking a little frustrated. "About that," he said. "Can we talk?"

Aphrodite glanced toward the sundial in the court-

154

yard. "Well, I'm kind of busy. I've got an extra-credit assignment to do to keep my grades up. But you can come with me if you want." She shut the doors, then headed into the Academy, and he followed her down the hall to an empty classroom.

Once inside, Ares glanced around the room, looking confused. "I don't think I've ever been in here before," he said. "Why are there so many mirrors everywhere? And what's in all those boxes and jars on those shelves against the wall?"

A smile tugged at Aphrodite's lips as she grabbed one of the many life-size fake heads sitting on a nearby shelf. No, he probably hadn't been in here. "This is Ms. ThreeGraces' class," she told him.

"Oh, yeah. Beauty-ology, right? No wonder." Ares wandered over to the shelves. When he opened a box at random, a magic makeup brush popped out. As it hovered in midair, directly in front of his astonished blue eyes, its bristles curved into a question-mark shape.

"Huh?" he said, jerking his head back. "What does it want?"

"Instructions," Aphrodite said, giggling. "On how to do your face." It was kind of adorable to see him befuddled by all the girly stuff in here.

"Uh, no," Ares told the brush, backing away. "None for me, thanks."

The brush reared back in surprise. In its mind, if it had one, it probably thought that everyone should wear makeup. Bristles drooping, the brush whisked back inside its box, whereupon the lid magically snapped shut behind it.

Aphrodite sneaked a peek at herself in one of the room's many mirrors as she sat down at a table with the fake head. She primped a little, straightening her chiton and patting a stray lock of golden hair into place as Ares ambled around, looking at stuff.

"What was going on out there with Makhai and Kydoimos just now?" he asked casually. "They seemed happy about something, which usually spells trouble."

Aphrodite frowned into the mirror. Seeing little lines crop up at the corners of her mouth, she quickly adopted a neutral expression. "They got perfect scores on yesterday's Science-ology quiz," she told him as she studied the fake head on the table in front of her. Her extra-credit assignment was to design a "futuristic makeup look" using her imagination to envision what someone might wear a hundred years from now. Unfortunately, her imagination was feeling stretched at the moment.

"No way!" Ares snorted. "Those two couldn't study their way out of a papyrus bag."

"They bragged it was because of Athena's study groups," Aphrodite told him as she brushed powder onto her fake head's face. "But some people on my team think they must have cheated somehow."

"Probably," said Ares.

"Really?" Aphrodite asked, looking over. "You're not going to take their side? Figured you might since they're on your team."

Ares shrugged. "They're in my study group, but they've never once shown up." He drummed his fingertips on the tabletop. "If they're cheating, it's wrong. But they may not be the only ones. Everyone's getting desperate to win."

"Honestly, I'll be glad when this is over." With a sigh, Aphrodite turned back to her assignment. She worked quickly, smoothing orange shadow and lip gloss on the dummy face in a dramatic way. Then she stroked a long thick swoop of purple liner on both upper eyelids and added black triangles above and below the eyes. The idea that competing for grades could lead to cheating had never occurred to her before, but now that she thought about it . . .

"She's gotten bigger. Have you noticed?" Ares stopped drumming. Hopping up, he shoved his hands in the pockets of his tunic and began to pace the room.

She shot him a quick glance, then added some glitter to her fake head. "Who?"

"My sister. You know how in nature some animals can puff themselves up to appear more formidable? Cats? Toads? When she starts feeling more and more powerful, Eris gets bigger like that. Not huge or anything, but she's at least a half-foot taller than usual now, and less scrawny. The ability is more unconscious than conscious, but when it happens, it definitely adds to her intimidation skills."

"Ye gods," said Aphrodite, pausing in her work to stare at him. "You almost sound . . . *afraid* of her."

He came to sit next to her. "Yeah, I know I'm the god-boy of war and I'm all about bravery and combat, but you don't know Eris like I do. All the arguing around here? The fighting? That's her."

Aphrodite's eyes widened. "You mean she's *causing* it? How? Why?"

"I told you she's the goddess of strife and discord at my party, remember? Trouble is what she does."

"Well, yeah, you did. But I just didn't connect it to what's going on here at MOA, I guess. The whole time she's been here, I've spent all my time thinking of ways to keep my team's grades up!" It was finally sinking in that he really didn't want Eris here. And with good reason!

In an attempt to lighten his mood, since she could tell

he was upset, she turned the head she was working on toward him and asked, "So what do you think?"

His eyes widened as he gazed at her project uncertainly. "It's . . . um . . . kind of frightening, actually."

They both burst out laughing. "It is, isn't it?" she said. "My assignment was to come up with a futuristic makeup look. I guess the future looks kind of scary to me at the moment."

Ares came over to sit on the table next to her and the head, his blue eyes earnest. "You have nothing to be afraid of, I promise. This contest will be over soon, and even if your team doesn't win, what's one more trophy anyway?" He chuckled. "You know, I actually thought for a while that that trophy of Eris's might be enchanted. That it was making you and Athena want it."

"Really?" said Aphrodite. In the last few days, whenever Eris had stayed in her room, she'd let Aphrodite polish the trophy. And Aphrodite's desire to possess it had only grown stronger with time. What Ares had just suggested was troubling, but on some level it had occurred to her, too. *Had* the trophy enchanted her? And maybe Athena, too?

"Yeah," Ares went on. "But Eris let me hold the thing, and I realized it was just a regular trophy. Not magic at all."

"Oh," she said, relieved. Soon she hoped to possess that trophy forever, so she was glad Ares didn't think there was any reason to avoid it.

He reached for her hand and held it. "I miss hanging out like this. The way our friendship used to be. Before my sister showed up and started this whole contest thing."

"Me too," Aphrodite said. "But she has helped in a way, I suppose. Grades are going up because of her contest. "

Before he could reply, Dionysus appeared in the

162

doorway. "There you are!" he exclaimed when he spotted Ares. He looked around the room and then grinned. "Getting some beauty tips?" he asked Ares.

Ares let go of her hand and jumped up. "Godsamighty! We have study group before dinner. I almost forgot."

Dionysus straightened, nodding. "Good thing I found you. If we're late . . ." He drew a finger across his throat. "Let's just say Athena will get grumpy if she finds out we didn't go."

Ares looked back over his shoulder at Aphrodite as he made for the door. "Talk later?"

She nodded, still feeling troubled by all he'd said. Once the boys left the classroom, she quickly redid her makeup project to make it a little less frightening. Then she headed upstairs to the dorm to change her chiton before dinner. Not that it was dirty or anything,

She just liked wearing different outfits for different activities. In her opinion, there was nothing wrong with changing clothes several times a day!

On her way up, she met Athena and Persephone coming down. Both girls had been chatting away with their heads close together. But when they saw Aphrodite, they broke off talking. They nodded and smiled stiffly as they passed her by.

Aphrodite's heart sank. Was it too much to hope that her friendship with her three BFFs would return to normal with no hurt feelings once the grades competition ended? She hoped so.

But first her team needed to win the contest. And she needed to win that trophy!

8

Poor Sports

Ares

AFTER DINNER, ARES ZOOMED BACK TO THE
sports fields in his new winged sandals. Coach Triathlon
was holding the first of several special workouts tonight
for all the boys who'd signed up to participate in the
upcoming Temple Games.

Unfortunately, the tensions sparked by Eris's contest had carried over to the workout. Ares could hardly

believe it when a member of Aphrodite's team, the normally mild-mannered Eros—the godboy of love, for godness' sake—elbowed Makhai in the side, pushing him out of his lane as they and several others competed in a race.

Apparently, the accusations that he and Kydoimos had cheated on the Science-ology quiz hadn't gone away. Soon guys from both sides were facing off and having yet another shouting match.

"We know you cheated!" Poseidon yelled at Makhai.

"Yeah," shouted Eros. "We just don't know how yet!"

"Leave Makhai alone!" Apollo yelled back. "You're only jealous because Athena's a better leader so our team is ahead!"

"Right on!" someone else chimed in. "Just a bunch of losers on Aphrodite's team!"

Ares stepped between the two groups. It was getting weird around here when the godboy of war was the one settling all the fights, but his sister's ability to cause discord never affected him as it did everyone else. So it looked like it was up to him to prevent all-out war during practice for the Temple Games!

"Hey, now," he shouted. "Can't we all just get along— *oomph!*"

Hades plowed into him, having been pushed from behind. Soon everyone was pushing and shoving everyone else.

"Stop that! Right now!" Blowing on his whistle, an angry and red-faced Coach Triathlon came running over from another part of the field, where he'd been setting up a climbing net as part of the obstacle course. He quickly rounded the students up and made them sit in the grassy area in the center of the track.

"Would someone explain to me what's going on here?" he yelled in a voice that was almost as loud as

Principal Zeus's. Apparently, he hadn't yet linked the ill will among the guys to the all-school grades contest, thought Ares. Though maybe he didn't know about that, since only academic grades counted.

When no one volunteered to explain, the coach went on to lecture them all about the importance of good sportsmanship. "Sometimes you'll win and sometimes you'll lose," he told them. "But a good sport respects his opponent, plays fair, and enjoys the game, whatever the outcome."

Ares had heard this speech before. More than once. He glanced around at the others. They'd all heard it too, and he wasn't sure how much of what the coach was saying was sinking in this time. Most of them were still scowling as they broke up later to work out on the obstacle course.

And not long afterward, when he and Heracles were

scrambling up the ropes of the first obstacle—the climbing net the coach had just set up—a stray discus almost beaned Heracles in the head.

"Sorry!" Atlas yelled from across the field, but there was a note of satisfaction in his voice.

"Yeah, right! I'll make you sorry!" Heracles said, shaking a fist in the air. Then, looking at Ares, he muttered, "That Atlas has been pushing my buttons a little too hard."

Heracles wasn't exactly acting even-tempered right now either, but Ares had about used up all the energy he had for that subject. As the two of them scaled the net wall, Ares's muscles bulged and his breath huffed out. "Hey, you know how you were wondering if Eris's trophy . . . could be putting . . . Athena and Aphrodite . . . under some kind of enchantment . . . to make them . . . mega-competitive?"

"Yeah?" said Heracles.

"I started to wonder . . . if you could be right."

They leaped to the ground and ran to the next obstacle, a series of magical hoops lying flat on the grass. The object was to quickly move across them, stepping *in* each hoop but not *on* them. They started across.

"And?" asked Heracles. "Athena's acting different . . . There's got to be some reason . . ."

"Not the trophy, though . . . Turns out it was just . . . a regular . . . trophy," Ares explained, his breath still huffing. The hard part of this obstacle was that the hoops moved, so you had to chase them down sometimes. "I held it . . . To see for myself . . . No magic in it, though," he went on as they both hopped around. Each time they successfully stepped inside a hoop, it lit up. The two boys finished the hoops and ran for the next obstacle.

"So, I guess . . . we were barking up the wrong tree,"

Heracles went on as they scaled a rope ladder up one side of a tree, then down the other.

"Ha-ha . . . I get it," said Ares, grinning at Heracles' joke. Heracles grinned back.

After dropping to the ground, the boys began to crawl over the grass on their bellies under a low-hanging net. "Your sister is . . . pretty intense," Heracles said as they scooted along. "Is it true . . . she's the goddess of strife and discord?"

Ares shot him a questioning look, and Heracles answered simply, "Pheme."

Ares nodded. He dug his elbows and knees into the ground to scramble forward faster. Without going into the embarrassing details of his childhood, he said, "Yeah, it's true." His breath was coming in superharsh snatches now, as the boys slid and crawled their way along the course.

Eventually, they reached the end of their crawl. Jumping to their feet, they ran to a weight-lifting station. Ares grabbed a barbell with fifty-pound weights on either end and began pumping it over his head. Grunting breathlessly between lifts, he said, "Eris gets . . . more powerful . . . by making trouble . . . like with this grades contest."

"Huh," Heracles grunted in reply. Instead of just *one* one-hundred-pound barbell, he was pumping *four*, two in each hand, and without even breaking a sweat. He was so strong that the barbells could have been toothpicks with marshmallows stuck on either end for all the effort he was using to lift them. Ares wasn't as strong as his friend, but on the other hand, he *could* outrace him.

THONK! Heracles set down all four barbells, then asked, "Think Zeus knows how this competition is affecting everyone?"

Ares frowned, dropping his too. "Nu-uh. So far, I think he's got tunnel vision. For him, it's all about improving our grades."

Coach Triathlon blew his whistle just then, signaling the end of practice. "Atlas, Apollo, Makhai, Eros, Poseidon!" he shouted. "You five stay behind and put all the equipment away."

It probably wasn't any accident that he'd asked those particular guys to stay, thought Ares. Anger was still sizzling between them, and Coach must've decided it would be good for them to have to work together under his direct supervision. As Ares and Heracles began walking back toward the Academy, Ares glanced over his shoulder to see that the coach was lecturing the five guys about good sportsmanship some more as they lugged equipment around.

When he and Heracles stepped into the MOA

courtyard, Ares spotted four girls at the far end of it practicing cheer. Aphrodite, Athena, Persephone, and Artemis. He and Heracles waved, but the girls weren't looking their way.

"Uh-oh," said Heracles, nudging him. Ares glanced over to see that Aphrodite and Athena had stopped leaping around like the others. They appeared to be arguing.

Ares made a move in their direction, but Heracles grabbed his arm. "God-dude!" he said, shaking his head. "Bad idea."

"You don't think we should try to help?" said Ares.

"And get them all mad at us, too? No thanks." Heracles let go of his arm.

Ares's brow furrowed, but he could see the wisdom in what Heracles had said. "I'll be glad when this contest is over," he muttered as they crossed the courtyard. "I don't even care which team wins."

"Me neither," said Heracles. He glanced back at the girls. "I just can't believe Athena's acting like this. Or Aphrodite. Something's come over them." They'd reached the Academy's bronze doors. "Hey, I'm going to hit the cafeteria for a snack before I go up," Heracles said, pulling the doors open.

Ares nodded, only half listening. "Later, then." As he took the stairs to the fifth floor. Heracles' words were echoing inside his head. *Something's come over them. Something's come over them.* Halfway down the dorm hall to his room, he suddenly remembered what Eris had actually replied when he'd asked if her trophy was enchanted: "You just said it felt like a plain ol' trophy to you. So I hope you're satisfied."

"It felt like a plain ol' trophy to you." A plain ol' trophy to . . . *him!* Him—a guy. And probably to other guys, as

well. But maybe for some unknown reason it was more than that to girls!

It had been a trick answer. Eris hadn't *exactly* lied about the enchantment. She just hadn't been completely truthful. Question was, now that he knew what he thought he knew, what could he do about it?

9

Meow!

Aphrodite

AFTER CHEER PRACTICE APHRODITE STOMPED upstairs to the girls' dorm, steaming mad. She and Athena had gotten into a big argument over nothing just now. Over a silly cheer move. Artemis and Persephone had tried to calm things down, but finally they'd just ended practice early. Her stomach was all jumpy now, and she felt horrible that she was on the outs with one of her best friends. That never happened! Till recently.

What was going on around here? she wondered as she threw open the door to her room. Lately, she hardly knew herself at times. Could Eris's influence as the goddess of strife and discord truly be affecting her behavior? She didn't think so. But it was almost like one of Pandora's trouble bubbles had bonked her again, changing her personality. Only that box of troubles was long gone now. So that couldn't be it. Must be the stress of this contest, that's all.

Hey! Her eyes narrowed. Maybe Athena was trying to upset her on purpose so she wouldn't be able to study. They both had a quiz this Friday in their first-period Hero-ology class. And naturally, Athena would want to get the best possible score on it since that would be the last day of the contest. And it wouldn't hurt if Aphrodite's score was subpar because she'd been too wound up to study, right? Opening her closet, she carefully stashed her pom-poms in their box on the shelf. She was mad, but that didn't mean she was going to be messy!

Mew! Adonis had awakened from his nap on her bed and padded over to see her. "Hi there, cutie," Aphrodite said to him as she sat down at her desk. She grabbed her Hero-ology textscroll and a pen. After opening the scroll with one hand, she dangled the pink feather end of her pen over the side of her chair. Adonis went wild, batting at the feather with his snowy white front paws and making her giggle.

"I've missed you," she crooned to him. Which was so true! Because the normally friendly kitten disliked Eris so much, and because Eris was spending every other night here with Aphrodite, Persephone had been keeping him at her house ever since Ares's party.

"It was so nice of Persephone to bring you for a sleepover with me tonight, sweetie petey," she cooed, lifting the kitten onto her desk. Eris was sleeping in Athena's room tonight, so the coast was clear for her to keep him.

Absently, she played with the kitten as she tried to study. But her thoughts kept returning to the contest. To pull a win out of the bag—and win the trophy out of Eris's bag—*her* team was going to have to do really, *really* well between now and Friday. Athena's team was ahead. Only by a few points. Still, it had her worried.

"Think I should have organized my team into study groups like Athena?" she asked Adonis. He rolled onto his back so she could rub his white tummy. "Too late now, anyway, with only two days to go. Maybe my pep talk earlier today will motivate them to step up their study efforts the next couple of days, though, right?" She sure hoped her team members weren't as stressed out as she was from all the tension around MOA.

Sighing she picked up Adonis and set him on her spare bed to take a nap. Back at her desk, she forced herself to concentrate on her textscroll and study notes.

Two hours later, the door flew open. Startled, Aphrodite looked up as Eris barged in without knocking.

"Pandora and Medusa had a little tiff or something, so Pandora's back with Athena tonight," Eris informed her. "Which means you and I are roomies again till Friday. Hope you don't mind." Without even looking around, she tossed the bag containing her trophy onto Aphrodite's spare bed.

Adonis reacted to Eris's arrival—and her bag almost landing on top of him!—with a loud scaredy-cat screech. *"ME-OW!"* He leaped from the bed to Aphrodite's desk to the shelf above it, knocking off two bottles of nail polish.

"Adonis! You're back!" Eagerly, Eris reached up to grab him.

Sssst! The kitten arched his back and hissed until she withdrew her hands. Looking freaked out, he took a series of jumps over to Aphrodite's bed, then burrowed under the coverlet to hide.

"Don't be a fraidy cat, Adonis! Calm down," Aphrodite scolded in a soft voice. Going over to her bed, she gave him a pat through the covers.

"S'okay," Eris said, shaking her head. But there was hurt in her voice as she added, "I have a bad effect on animals." Then she added more quietly, "And people, too. I had a few friends at Corinthian, though. Before the roof incident, anyway." The word "incident" made Aphrodite smile to herself.

"What?" asked Eris, frowning at her.

"Oh, nothing," said Aphrodite. She went back to her

desk to roll up her textscroll and stow it away. Glancing over her shoulder at Eris, she said, "It's just that my friends tease me about that word—'incident.' Apparently, I use it for every occasion, from something that happens at a party to something that starts a war."

A smile tugged at Eris's lips. As she shifted her black bag so she could sit on the spare bed, a blue letterscroll with her name on it in big block letters slid out and onto the floor, drawing both their gazes.

"What's that?" Aphrodite asked. "A message from some admirer, perhaps?" As the goddessgirl of love, she was always on the lookout for signs of romance. Though in this case she was probably way off base. Given Eris's troublesome nature, not many boys would likely be drawn to her.

However, to Aphrodite's surprise, Eris blushed. Then, recovering herself, she snapped, "It's nothing.

Just because you're the goddessgirl of love, don't suppose there's love everywhere you look!" After grabbing the letterscroll, she stuffed it back in her bag. Then she took out the trophy and began to polish it.

The second she caught sight of the trophy, Aphrodite's fingers itched to hold it. However, for the first time, she noticed that Eris herself seemed enamored of the trophy too. She wasn't going to change her mind about giving it away as a prize, Aphrodite hoped. Maybe she was just polishing it now to soothe herself after Adonis's rejection. Though she'd acted as if she was used to that kind of thing happening, it still had to hurt. Everyone wanted to be liked. Especially by babies and pets. It would certainly hurt *her* feelings, not to mention embarrass her, if Adonis treated her like he did Eris.

She wondered what it would be like to *be* Eris, feeding on turmoil and strife most of the time. Seemed like it would make a person unhappy. Miserable, in fact. And people who feel miserable sometimes create misery for others. Kind of a vicious cycle.

Aphrodite left her desk and went to sit cross-legged on her bed, opposite Eris on the spare one. She put one hand on the lump that was Adonis and petted him through the covers. With her other hand, she grabbed a heart-shaped red pillow and hugged it to her chest.

"So what did you do today?" she asked Eris brightly. Maybe she could make up for Adonis's rejection by giving the girl some positive attention. In all the turmoil lately, she hadn't had much chance to buddy up to Ares's sister as she'd originally intended to. She still held out hope they'd become more sisterly.

Eris just kept rubbing the golden apple at the top of the trophy until it shone as bright as a torchlight. "Keeping track of team scores takes time," was all she said. "I told you that Athena's team is several points ahead of yours, right?"

Aphrodite clutched the pillow she held more tightly and nodded as worry filled her once more. Had she studied enough for Friday's test? Should she go around the dorm and spot-check that her team members were studying for their tests too?

"So what do you think?" Eris asked, holding the gleaming trophy out to Aphrodite at last. "Really awesome, isn't it?"

Aphrodite dropped the pillow and eagerly reached out. As soon as she grasped the trophy, her desire to possess it forever seized her anew. "It really is the most beautiful trophy imagineable," she crooned. "Oh, I just *have* to win it!"

Running her fingers back and forth over the words "For the Fairest," she gazed dreamily at an empty spot she'd cleared on her shelf. She planned to display the golden apple trophy there where she could see it every morning when she woke up. Or maybe Principal Zeus would want to put it in a place of honor in the display case down on the first floor of the school. No! Then she wouldn't be able to hold it and—

"I'm tired. Let's hit the sack," said Eris. When she snatched the trophy back, Aphrodite felt an overwhelming sense of loss.

Eris bent to stuff the trophy back in her bag. *"Rip!"* At the small sound, a tear appeared in the seam of the chiton she wore. It was the cotton-candy pink one that Aphrodite had worn especially for Ares's birthday party. It used to be one of her favorite chitons, but now there were a half dozen similar rips in it. She remembered that her chitons had all seemed a bit large and long on Eris the first few days she'd worn them. However, now every one of them seemed a little too tight and short.

Her gaze met Eris's. The girl's eyes were gleaming even brighter than the trophy! And it seemed to Aphrodite that Ares's sister grew a couple of inches taller right then and there. It was her sense of power that fed her growth, Ares had said. Did that mean she thought she had some power over Aphrodite?

When Aphrodite awoke the next morning, she was lying on her back and Adonis was sitting on top of her, cleaning his soft white paws. He'd spent the whole night in her bed, probably so she'd "protect" him from Eris.

"Morning, cuddlykins. Just one more day till we win that trophy-wophy," she cooed to him. Hugging him, she stared at the empty spot on her shelf again.

Eris was already gone. The spare bed was a mess, covers half off the mattress and pillows every which way. After cleaning Adonis's cat box and filling his water bowl from the bathroom sink down the hall, Aphrodite poured fresh cat food into his food bowl. Then, with a sigh, she cleaned up the mess Eris had left behind: crumpled chitons strewn on the closet floor and, scattered across her spare desk, open pots of makeup and a spilled bottle of nail polish.

"See you later, cutie wootie," she sang out to Adonis as she left for breakfast a half hour later. After blowing him a kiss, she started down the hall.

"Hey, Aphrodite, wait up!" Ares called to her as she moved down the marble staircase a minute later. She watched him take the stairs two at a time from the boys' dorm a floor above. When he caught up to her, he announced, "I think that trophy of my sister's is enchanted after all!"

"What?" scoffed Aphrodite. "That's crazy. You held it yourself and said it was just a regular trophy, remember?" Flipping a hand as if to brush away the silly notion, she continued downstairs.

"No, listen," Ares said, keeping pace with her. "It's the only thing that makes sense. It's true it had no effect on me. But why else would you and Athena be so gaga over it?"

"Gaga? I don't think so." The notion nagged at her mind, but she pushed it away at the same time that she pushed a lock of her golden hair back over one shoulder. "Anyway, how can you blame us? It's the most amazing trophy I've ever seen. The way it gleams. That apple. In fact, it's the most enchanting—" She broke off in confusion when she realized she'd been about to use essentially the same word Ares had just used to describe the trophy.

Ares gave her a crooked smile. "Yeah, exactly. I think its enchantment only works on girls, though. Girls who touch it. You and Athena."

Hmm, mused Aphrodite. But no! She didn't *want* him to be right about the enchantment. She just wanted the trophy to be hers, and she didn't want him spoiling that. "Then why doesn't it work on Eris?" she countered. "She touches it all the time."

Ares shrugged. "I'm not sure."

Even as he said this, however, Aphrodite was remembering how enamored Eris had seemed of the trophy last night as she was polishing it. At the time Aphrodite had thought the girl was only consoling herself after Adonis's rejection, but if the trophy really *was* enchanted, maybe it was having an effect on her, too, though she might not be aware of it.

"Hmm," she said, considering Ares's idea. "During your birthday party, Hera picked it up, too. By accident, though. Eris didn't invite her to hold it like she did Athena and me." Had Hera also been affected? That might explain her strange behavior during the party, Aphrodite thought uneasily, remembering how Hera had insisted on joining the students' game. How she'd seemed determined to win the trophy for herself.

"Has anyone else touched it?" Ares asked.

Aphrodite slowly shook her head. "At your party Persephone asked me if she could hold it. I hesitated to let her. Before I could change my mind, Eris grabbed the trophy from me and stashed it away." Ares's suspicions began to seem more and more plausible. "But why would your sister target Athena and me with her trophy?" she asked, confused and also a little hurt.

"Maybe because I like you and she wants to punish me for being invited to attend MOA when she wasn't. And Athena is Principal Zeus's daughter. Even though I think Eris admires Zeus, maybe she can't help being mad at him, too, for not inviting her to enroll at MOA all these years. What better way to punish both Zeus and me than by creating trouble between the two of you?"

"I guess you're saying makes sense," Aphrodite admitted reluctantly. "In fact, I've noticed that when I don't touch the trophy for a while, I don't care about it so much. But then Eris offers to let me hold it again, and suddenly the wanting is stronger." She stopped on the stairs and looked at him. "I hate to admit it," she said, "but I think you are right!"

"So maybe the trophy's power to enchant loses some strength over time and has to be refreshed with a touch," Ares said, as they continued on down.

"I'd better tell Athena about this," said Aphrodite.

"Yeah and Heracles, too," said Ares. "Let's find them."

They sped up, hurrying for the cafeteria now. When they arrived, Ares pulled open the door and . . . *splat!*

Someone hit him right in the face with an ambrosia

cream pie! In fact, the entire cafeteria was a mess, with students hurling bits of breakfast and snack foods this way and that.

Aphrodite ducked as a carton of nectar sailed over her head. It slammed into the door behind her and exploded, splashing nectar everywhere. Luckily, her chiton didn't get wet. Ares hadn't been so lucky, though. There was pie dripping down the neck of his tunic.

"What the—?" he yelled. But some of the pie must have made it into his mouth, because then he licked his lips. "Mmm. That's pretty good," he murmured.

"FOOD FIGHT!" Heracles yelled, racing up to them. He shoved a basketful of pastries into Ares's arms. "Have some ammo!" he shouted over the noisy hubbub that filled the room.

"Thanks!" Ares shouted back. And just like that, he was drawn into the fight.

"Wait!" Aphrodite called. "What about the trophy? What about telling Athena and Heracles?" But Ares was already gone, swallowed up in the brawl.

Athena spotted Artemis in the thick of the action too. But her dogs seemed to be having more fun than anyone, delightedly scarfing up every scrap of food that landed on the floor.

Well, good for them, thought Aphrodite. However, she had no wish to spoil her hair or her chiton, thank you very much. Quickly, she looked around for Athena.

"Over here!" called a voice. It was Persephone! She and Athena were crouched underneath the table where they, Aphrodite, and Artemis usually sat at lunch.

Skirting a gloppy slick of oatmeal, then ducking just in time to miss getting nailed with a wad of nectaroni, Aphrodite somehow managed to safely make her way over to them. She huddled under the table too, staring out at all the chaos.

"What started this?" she asked.

"We don't know," said Persephone.

"Seemed like tensions just sort of exploded, and then everyone was throwing food," Athena added.

"It probably has something to do with Eris!" Aphrodite proceeded to share Ares's theory about the trophy and why only Athena and herself had been encouraged to touch it. And how Eris had a troublemaking effect wherever she went.

As she spoke, Athena's blue-gray eyes widened. "Ye gods!" she exclaimed. "If you guys are right, that would explain a lot. Heracles keeps telling me I'm obsessed with that trophy, but until now, I didn't really believe it."

"Yeah, I've been obsessed with it too," Aphrodite admitted. "Still am, really. Even though I know it has probably enchanted me, I still want it. But maybe the feeling will fade if we don't touch it again."

Athena nodded. "Okay, I'll try not to." But then she frowned. "You're not just saying that so I won't want it, are you? So you can have it for yourself?"

"What? You don't even trust me, your own friend?" Aphrodite retorted hotly.

"Wait, you guys! Listen to what you're saying," Persephone urged. "You are not yourselves. You've been trophy-tized. As in hypnotized by an enchanted trophy!"

"Sorry," said Athena.

Aphrodite nodded. "Yeah, me too." She peeked out to see if she could find Ares. However, she spotted Eris instead. She was standing in a corner of the cafeteria farthest from the action, cradling the trophy in her arms. And she was also wearing another of Aphrodite's pink chitons. A frilly one, with satin bows at the neck and hem. And, as usual, she hadn't asked to borrow it. She looked serenely happy as she gazed at the mayhem going on around her.

Before Aphrodite could point her out to the others, a red-faced Mr. Cyclops burst through the open door of the cafeteria. He was a long way from the Hero-ology classroom where he taught.

"A cafeteria lady must've summoned him," said Persephone, sounding relieved.

"This has gone far enough!" Mr. Cyclops shouted just as Ares chucked a frosted ambrosia fritter at Eros. Unfortunately, the Titan-tall teacher was standing directly behind Apollo. And Ares had aimed too high. *Whap!* The fritter nailed Mr. Cyclops square on the forehead just above his single eye. Frosting goo went sliding down his face.

"I said ENOUGH!" Mr. Cyclops bellowed. Instantly, the food stopped flying.

198

"Sorry!" Ares said meekly into the sudden quiet.

But the teacher didn't hear. "Who started this?" he demanded. His big eyeball swept the room.

For a moment no one volunteered an answer. But then, eyes gleaming, Eris sidled over to the teacher and whispered something to him. She was even taller than Ares now!

"Is it my imagination, or has Eris gained weight? And gotten taller?" said Persephone.

The hem of the floor-length pink-striped chiton she wore—another of Aphrodite's favorites—barely covered her knees and was tight.

"Yeah. Seems like it," said Athena. "Maybe she's been working out at the gym every day during classes? But that wouldn't explain her getting taller."

"It's part of her goddess talent," Aphrodite explained quickly. "Ares told me she's the goddess of strife and discord. And she feeds off of the power thrill she gets from causing trouble."

"Yeah, I heard about her goddess title. But I didn't know she could actually feed off troublemaking," said Persephone. "She must be loving this. The cafeteria is a wreck!"

Athena looked at Aphrodite a bit sheepishly. "She almost wrecked our friendship, too."

"But she didn't," said Aphrodite. Grinning, she punched a fist in the air. "Down with trophy-tizing, I say!"

When Athena and Persephone laughed, Aphrodite held up a hooked pinky finger toward each of them. "GGBFFs forever?"

Athena and Persephone caught her pinkies with theirs and they looped pinkies together too. "Yes! Pinky swear," they all promised.

"Aphrodite! Ares! Athena! Heracles!" Mr. Cyclops

barked out. "You four report to Principal Zeus's office. Immediately!"

Huh? thought Aphrodite as the three girls jumped apart. She looked around for Eris, but the girl had disappeared. "When she whispered to Mr. Cyclops, she must have pinned the blame for the food fight on us!" Aphrodite told Athena.

"Great," Athena replied, sighing.

As Ares and Heracles crossed the cafeteria to the door, Athena and Aphrodite dutifully scrambled out from beneath their table and went to join their crushes at the door. Aphrodite was both hurt and furious at Eris's likely betrayal. She'd been *nice* to that girl. She'd wanted to be like sisters with her. She'd shared her room and let Eris borrow her chitons and use her makeup. She'd even cleaned up after the girl! And how did Eris pay her back? By trying to get her in trouble! *Grrr.*

As Aphrodite, Athena, Ares, and Heracles hesitated near the door, Mr. Cyclops roared, "Get going, you four. Now!"

"Don't worry," Ares said to Aphrodite as they started toward Principal Zeus's office. "We'll make Zeus understand that my sister's the one who's really responsible for that food fight. And we'll get him to put a stop to this competition."

"I hope so," Aphrodite told him, though she had her doubts about that.

What if Zeus was so pleased with the rise in grades that he was on Eris's side? And what if they couldn't convince him that contest tensions were the true cause of the food fight? Maybe he'd even decide to *extend* the competition. And let Eris enroll at the Academy!

10

A Few Complaints

Ares

ALL NINE OF MS. HYDRA'S HEADS LOOKED UP from her tall desk when Ares and the other three students entered the front office. "Mr. Cyclops sent us here to talk to Principal Zeus about the—" he started to say.

"The food fight?" Ms. Hydra's gossipy pink head interrupted to finish. "Yes, I heard about it. Did Mr. Cyclops really get hit in the face with a nectar jelly doughnut?"

"Actually," Ares put in, "it was a frosted ambrosia fritter." How had she found out so fast?

Aphrodite, Athena, and Heracles stared at him. Too late, he realized that what he'd just said was almost as good as a confession. Because only the person who'd thrown the pastry would be likely to know for sure what it was.

"Hooligans," muttered Ms. Hydra's grumpy green head.

Her sympathetic blue head just clucked its tongue. "I hope you don't get into too much trouble. Or expelled."

Expelled? He saw Aphrodite and Athena exchange looks of horror. He was pretty horrified by the possibility too. You just never knew with Zeus. Would he be understanding and helpful, or angry and in thunderbolt-throwing punishment mode?

Ms. Hydra's efficient gray head pushed the guest book across the desk toward them. "Sign in, please.

Principal Zeus has a visitor right now. But he can see you in a few—"

Just then, the door to the principal's inner office was flung open so hard it ripped loose from one of its hinges to hang at an angle. Since Zeus constantly misjudged his own strength, this happened a lot, of course, but especially when he was in a bad mood. Like now. His brows were drawn together and his muscles bulged, electric sparks popping from all over his skin.

Pheme scurried out of the inner office ahead of the principal as he stood to one side of his wobbly door.

Well, that explained Zeus's bad mood, thought Ares. Pheme had probably used those orange wings of hers to zip up here from the cafeteria to tell the principal and Ms. Hydra about the food fight two seconds after Mr. Cyclops ordered Ares and the others to the office. This goddessgirl of gossip liked to be the first to spread news.

However, she often got some of the details wrong—like the type of pastry that had hit Mr. Cyclops in the eye. Ares wondered what else Pheme had gotten wrong in what she'd told Zeus.

Of course, whether the Hero-ology teacher had been hit by a jelly doughnut or a frosted fritter would make no difference. If the principal was of a mind to punish the perpetrators of the food fight, he'd do just that. And though neither Ares nor Heracles had started the fight, they had been involved in it. He braced for the worst.

Pheme's orange-glossed lips had twisted into a grimace of concern when she saw the four students waiting. "Good luck," she mouthed as she fluttered past them.

Zeus glowered at them. "YOU FOUR! ENTER!" he boomed. Everyone ducked as a spark of electricity shot from his fingertips. *Zzzt!* It hit the wall behind Ms. Hydra's desk and harmlessly fizzled out. Her heads were so used to such things by now, none of them even bothered to glance over.

Ares led the way as he and his companions headed to their doom. Behind them, he heard Ms. Hydra on the intercom, summoning a custodian to fix Zeus's door. It happened so often, they probably stocked boxes of replacement hinges in the supply closet.

As usual, the inside of Zeus's office was a mess. His filing cabinet, which he often used as a barbell, lay tipped over on its side in the middle of the floor, and they all had to walk around it to cross the room. Ares almost tripped over an empty, smashed can of Zeus Juice and a discarded Thunderbolt Crunch cereal box as he and the others made their way to the row of chairs facing the principal's enormous desk.

"SIT!" Zeus barked at them when they stood before his desk.

Ares swept several Opposite-Oracle-O cookie wrappers and the lid to an Olympus-opoly game off the seat of a padded blue chair and sat between Aphrodite and Heracles. His chair had scorch marks on its cushions, like all the chairs in Zeus's office. Just how many students had been *sitting* in the very same blue chair each time it got zapped was a question he preferred not to think about.

Zeus moved behind his desk. As he lowered himself onto his huge golden throne, Ares couldn't help noticing a large abstract painting done in shades of white, blue, and brown on the wall to the right of the throne. No, wait, he thought, studying it more closely. It wasn't an abstract after all, but a poorly executed picture of . . . *something*. A cloud? A gob of ambrosia? Though Ares was no artist himself, this painting looked to have been done by a five-year-old using finger paints. He noticed the others were staring at it too.

"Like it?" Zeus asked, brightening as he followed their gazes. He hooked a thumb over his shoulder at the picture. "Did it myself. Been feeling kind of tense lately, so I needed a creative outlet."

Aphrodite nodded. "Good idea, Principal Zeus. You've really captured something."

"I agree, Dad," Athena added quickly. "Good job."

Had Zeus been tense because of Eris's presence at MOA? Ares immediately wondered. He didn't ask. Instead he commented on the picture too. "Yeah, the lines just seem to . . . um . . . *gallop* across the painting."

"Totally," Heracles put in.

Zeus sprea both arms wide and beamed at the godboys. "Exactly what I was going for!" he said. "Pegasus in action!"

Ares struggled to keep his face from betraying his surprise. *Pegasus? Zeus's winged horse?* That was what the painting was supposed to show?

"See?" said Zeus, pointing. "He's flying above the roof of the Academy."

"Yeah, sure. It's genius," Ares fibbed. The others added admiring comments as well.

"Thanks," Zeus replied modestly. Then a frown came over his face, as if he'd just remembered why they were here. After shoving aside several issues of a scrollazine titled *Great Principals Quarterly*, he plucked a papyrus scroll from a stack of papers on his desk. "Aha! Here it is."

Snap! He gave the scroll a single hard shake, causing it to unroll. "Look at this," he said, holding the chart up so all four students could see. It was a vertical bar graph, showing the results of the competition so far. What did that have to do with the food fight? Ares wondered. Well, the contest did have something to do with it, actually, but Zeus didn't know that, did he?

"This chart shows total points per team in the

210

grades competition." Zeus pointed to the tallest bar, which was colored red. "Red is Theeny's team," he said, using his nickname for Athena. Then he pointed to the blue bar next to it, which was only a tiny bit shorter. "Blue is your team, Aphrodite."

"What are those two green bars next to the red and blue ones?" Athena asked. The green bars were only about half the height of the other two.

"The green bars," Zeus said grandly, "represent the lower projected team scores that MOA students *would* have made, based on quizzes and tests over the last two weeks, if Eris hadn't come to the Academy. Overall, grade point averages have increased by fifty percent, as you can see from the red and blue bars."

Heracles gave a low whistle. "Wow. That's incredible!"

"Great," Athena and Aphrodite said at the same time.

"Yeah," Ares agreed, but with a sinking feeling in the

pit of his stomach. With this kind of success, Eris was that much closer to getting the permanent place at MOA that she wanted so badly.

Zeus dropped the chartscroll back on top of his stack of papers. "Great? It's stupendous!" he declared. Then a cloud came over his face and he slammed a fist on his desk. "And I don't want anything to happen that could undermine these results."

"If you're referring to that food fight," Ares dared to say. "We didn't start it—"

"Yeah, I mean, Ares did throw that fritter," Heracles put in, "but he was aiming for Eros, and—" He stopped, looking flustered.

"—and it was actually Eris that—" Athena started to say.

"Yeah, she—" Aphrodite said over the top of Athena.

Bam! Zeus slammed his big hammy fist down on the desktop even harder, making his stack of papers fly and all four students jump. "Enough about the food fight!" he thundered. "Pheme told me all about it. Said it was already in progress before you four entered the cafeteria. Said it was impossible to know who really started it."

He paused, eyeing them carefully. "I had Mr. Cyclops send you here so I could ask you to help keep a lid on any more trouble until final grades are in on Friday."

Huh? Ares looked at his friends, seeing the same confusion on their faces.

As often happened, Zeus's mood abruptly changed lightning fast. Suddenly he was all smiles again. "And speaking of Eris," he said to Ares. "When it comes to improved academic results, your sister is the best thing to ever happen to this school." His eyes lit up as he added, "And professionally speaking, she's done me a huge favor."

He tapped the top copy of *Great Principals Quarterly*, sending several sparks flying. Leaning forward, Aphrodite discreetly stamped out a spark that had landed on the floor with the toe of her pink sandal. Fortunately, the rest of the sparks sizzled out almost instantly.

Meanwhile, the principal produced a new can of Zeus Juice from his desk drawer and popped open the top.

"Such a huge increase in grades will help put me over the top when the editorial board of *Great Principals Quarterly* meets to name their very first Principal of the Year in just two more months," he gloated. Then he took a big glug of the juice.

Aha! thought Ares, as all had become clear. He should have known that Zeus would have a personal reason for wanting to keep Eris here these past two weeks despite the trouble she was causing among students. But did the principal really expect the four of them to somehow prevent further tensions? And if the editorial board of the scrollazine wasn't meeting to choose their Principal of the Year for two more months, did that mean—?

"So first thing this morning, before breakfast, I met with Eris and told her I've decided to continue the competition. Instead of ending it tomorrow," Zeus added, "it'll go on for another two months. Maybe longer. I'll likely be inviting her to enroll."

As Zeus took another big swig of Zeus Juice, Ares felt his insides seize up. He jumped to his feet. "No! You can't let her stay that long. She's got to go!"

Juice sprayed from Zeus's mouth and anger filled his face.

Uh-oh, Ares thought, sinking down to his seat again. You absolutely did not tell the King of the Gods and Ruler of the Heavens what he could or could not do. Not if you knew what was good for you, that is.

"And exactly why must she go?" Zeus demanded. At the same time, Athena leaped from her chair and ran from his office, returning seconds later with a cloth she must've gotten from Ms. Hydra.

"Because she's trouble with a capital *T*," Ares insisted as Athena began wiping the drips of juice from her dad's desktop. "Just her *presence* in the cafeteria was probably enough to spark that food fight!" Helped along by Heracles and the two girls, he told Zeus about all the bad feelings between students leading to the fights that had been going on lately.

"And the fighting's not just between team members. Even members of the *same* team are arguing," Athena added once she'd finished mopping up the juice.

Frowning, Zeus propped his feet on top of his desk and leaned back in his chair. His forehead wrinkled in thought as he steepled his fingers together on his chest.

"There *have* been a few complaints from teachers in the last few days," he admitted. "Coach Triathlon came to see me last night, in fact. He was concerned about contest tensions carrying over to the sports fields."

The principal's crossed feet began to wiggle in irritation atop his desk. "And Muse Urania is worried about students cheating. She said that the answer key to a recent Science-ology quiz she gave disappeared from her desk drawer." He shifted his weight on his throne. "I sent her back to her room to search again, figuring she'd just misplaced her answer key. She hasn't reported back to me, but just before you got here, a little bird told me there are a couple of suspects in the possible theft."

No need to guess who that "little bird" was, thought Ares. *Pheme, of course.*

"Suspects? You mean Makhai and Kydoimos?" Athena asked. Then her hand flew to cover her mouth. Ares figured that she hadn't meant for their names to slip out. The two boys were on her team, after all. Still, Athena wouldn't approve of them cheating.

Whomp! Zeus dropped his sandaled feet to the floor again. He leaned across his desk, arching an eyebrow at Athena. "You and the little bird seem to be in agreement concerning the culprits." He grabbed a sheet of papyrus from his desk. After scribbling a note on it, he folded it in quarters and motioned for Athena to take it from him.

"Give this to Ms. Hydra, please, Theeny. She'll know what to do with it."

Athena jumped from her chair to take it. Ares and the others stared after her as she left the office, though she was soon back again. Ares wondered what had been on that sheet of papyrus. That it had something to do with Makhai and Kydoimos seemed clear enough, however.

"There's another thing you should know," Aphrodite chimed in.

Zeus's blue eyes peered at her sharply. "Oh? What's that?" He stood and began to pace back and forth behind his desk, as if he couldn't take any more bad news sitting down.

"Eris has a special trophy," Aphrodite informed him. "And we think it's enchanted."

"But it seems to only affect girls," Heracles added.

"And *women*," Athena said. "Maybe even Hera. Like at Ares's birthday party. Remember how reluctant she was to stop playing that game?"

"A trophy?" Zeus echoed in surprise.

"She carries it around in that black bag of hers," Athena supplied.

"Oh?" said Zeus. "The black bag."

Eris hadn't shown the trophy inside her bag to him, Ares realized. Hera had seen it, but she must not have told Zeus about it.

Aphrodite was squirming in her chair. "The trophy's pull is hard to resist. Every time I touch it, I want it more," she admitted.

"Me too," Athena said earnestly.

A strange expression came over Zeus's face as they were telling him this. "Hmm," he said, pausing in mid-stride. "That might explain why Hera keeps asking me to invite Eris to have dinner with us and to make sure she brings her black bag with her when she comes."

"And *have* you invited her?" Athena asked, curious.

"Well, no," Zeus admitted.

"Why not, Dad?" she pressed.

Zeus fingered the neckline of his tunic. "Okay, you

caught me. I fear that Eris's very presence might spark a fight between Hera and me. Eris has that effect, you know."

 All four students stared at him. "We know!" Ares exclaimed.

"Yeah!" said Heracles.

"That's what we've been trying to tell you!" said Aphrodite.

Athena nodded.

"So maybe you could end the competition after all and send my sister back home?" Ares asked hopefully.

"No can do. I promised her from the start that she could attend MOA permanently if her contest increased grade point averages by at least twenty percent," said Zeus. "The results so far have beat all my expectations."

"Doesn't it matter that at least two students cheated to get good grades?" Heracles broke in to remind him.

"Those boys' disgraceful behavior will have consequences—" Zeus broke off to gaze longingly at his stack of *Great Principals Quarterly*. Was he worried that if he sent Eris home, grades would plummet and he might not make Principal of the Year? Ares wondered.

Seemed like the principal should be worrying more about Eris's troublemaking skills. But if he *did* dis-invite her to MOA, she wouldn't take kindly to being crossed. Not even by Zeus. She might even do as he feared and try to cause trouble between Hera and him. It was a real dilemma!

Appearing to reach a decision at last, Principal Zeus turned to face Ares. "She's *your* sister," he said craftily. "So I hereby command you to get her to declare a winner in the grades contest as soon as possible. And to convince her to go to school somewhere else."

Zeus is passing the buck to me? Ares thought in

shock. Was even the King of the Gods and Ruler of the Heavens just a little bit chicken when it came to dealing with his potentially vengeful sister? In a weird way, that notion was sort of comforting. Made Ares feel less like a chicken himself.

"But she doesn't listen to me," Ares protested anyway. "So maybe it would be better if—"

"Ahem," said Athena. Ares glanced over to see that she and Aphrodite were making frantic slashing motions across their throats to indicate that contradicting Zeus on this matter was not a good idea. And if he needed any more convincing, the thunderous scowl on Zeus's face provided it.

"—better if I found a way to change her mind," Ares finished wisely.

"That's the spirit!" Zeus declared, rubbing his hands together. He quickly ushered the foursome out of his office. "Well, off you go, and good luck. I need to start writing my acceptance speech for that Principal of the Year Award. Because now that I think about it, I'm still likely to win, regardless of what happens with the competition. Though student grades are important, who would dare deny the King of the Gods and the Ruler of the Heavens such an honor!" he crowed.

"I'm glad *somebody's* happy," Ares mumbled to the others as they all left his office.

"So what are you going to say to Eris to get her to end the competition and go home?" Aphrodite asked as the four of them started down the hall.

"No clue," Ares admitted. He'd just have to hope something would come to him. And that he could somehow contain his sister's fury when he did. Or else he'd need to start wearing that suit of armor from his dorm from now on to protect himself from those pinches of hers!

11

Up a Tree

Aphrodite

MAYBE WE'LL BE ABLE TO HELP YOU THINK OF
what to do if we eat something first," Aphrodite told
Ares as they left Zeus's office with Athena and Heracles.
"I don't know about you guys, but I'm starving. Because
of that food fight, I missed breakfast."

"Let's stop at the cafeteria before class," Athena
suggested. "We've pretty much missed first period, but

we've still got time before second period starts."

"Good idea," said Ares. "I could eat a horse. Not the one in Zeus's painting, though," he joked lamely.

Heracles rubbed his stomach. "Let's go. I'm starving too."

As they neared the cafeteria, the gooey remains of a nectar cupcake suddenly dropped from where it had been stuck to the ceiling to land on the floor in front of Aphrodite. Her arms windmilled as she tried to keep her balance and not step in it. Ares caught her arms and gallantly lifted her over the cupcake.

"My hero," she teased, but in a grateful tone. She kept a wary eye on the domed ceiling the rest of the way to the cafeteria. In case there were more cupcakes waiting to unstick themselves.

The ceilings throughout MOA were covered with paintings that never failed to impress her. Paintings that illustrated the glorious exploits of the gods and goddesses. One showed Zeus battling giants that were storming Mount Olympus, carrying torches and spears. Another showed him driving a chariot pulled by four white horses across the sky as he hurled thunderbolts into the clouds.

Whoever had painted that last scene had really managed to capture the force Zeus used in tossing those thunderbolts, Aphrodite thought. She smiled to herself, thinking that he would be an awesome ally in a food fight.

A lunch lady with a long snout like an anteater was nosing around the floor of the cafeteria as the foursome pushed through the doors. She was sucking up the last remaining crumbs from the fight. And looking green-faced and icked-out as they followed along behind her with wet mops were none other than Makhai and Kydoimos!

Athena leaned over to Aphrodite. "I'm guessing those are the consequences my dad mentioned. Pushing those mops."

Aphrodite nodded, trying not to smirk at the mop boys. They'd all seen that particular lunch lady in action on other occasions, but still. Ick. She managed to smile at the anteater lady, who gave her a wink and kept on with her work. Makhai and Kydoimos kept their heads down. For once, they had nothing to say.

Aphrodite and her three companions grabbed apples and pears from a huge fruit bowl on the snacks table and ambrosia muffins from a large platter.

As they headed out, munching the snacks, they passed Persephone. She was holding Adonis in her arms.

"Good. You're back," she said to them, sounding relieved. "Here's the news. Everyone else is still out in the courtyard, where Mr. Cyclops and the cafeteria ladies shooed us after the fight. I snuck in to get Adonis just now. Mom sent a note saying she needs to pick me up early, and it's my turn to take him. So is it true that Principal Zeus tried to expel all of you?" she finished breathlessly.

"No!" said Aphrodite.

"Oh, I'm so glad. That was just Pheme spreading her usual rumors, then," said Persephone as she led the way outside.

"There you are!" Artemis yelled when they appeared at the top of the granite steps and started down to the courtyard. She and her crush, Actaeon, had been tossing a ball for her three dogs. But now they and some others ran toward Aphrodite and her friends. As a group of students gathered around to listen, Aphrodite, Athena, Ares, and Heracles quickly explained most of what had gone on in Zeus's office.

Hades ran a hand through his dark curls and frowned. "I'll be glad to see this contest come to an end. There's too much bad feeling between—"

"Speaking of which," interrupted Ares, "has anyone seen Eris?"

Medusa, who was among the group listening, hooked a thumb over her shoulder toward the side of the courtyard. "I think she's in the olive grove. My snakes hissed at her when she passed by going that direction a few minutes ago."

Aphrodite, Ares, Athena, and Heracles exchanged glances. "Check you later," Ares announced to the gathered crowd. "We need to go have a word with my sister."

"I'll come too since my mom's not here yet," Persephone insisted, with Adonis still cuddled in her arms. Unlike most cats, Adonis loved being around noise and people and was napping away. "I'll see her chariot when it flies in," she added.

She, Aphrodite, Ares, Athena, and Heracles soon found Eris sitting on a bench in the olive grove. She was rereading the blue letterscroll that had fallen out of her bag the night before, Aphrodite noticed. As they approached, Eris looked up and saw them. Hurriedly, she stuffed the letterscroll back inside her bag.

"Heard about your little visit with Principal Zeus," she said to Ares with a smirk. "How did it go?" Obviously, Eris didn't know that her attempt to pin the blame for the food fight on the four of them had failed.

Aphrodite was relieved when Ares didn't rise to the bait. "Fine," he said evenly. "He's very pleased with your contest results, by the way."

Eris's smirk wavered and she leaped to her feet. She seemed unsure if she should take her brother's remark as a compliment—or as a veiled insult. It wasn't just her smirk that wavered, either. Aphrodite could have sworn that the girl's height yo-yoed up and down with her uncertainty, too.

Sweeping the group with a belligerent look, Eris said, "I bet none of you thought I could raise the grades so quickly."

"Why would you think that?" Aphrodite started to protest.

But Ares cut in. "You've always been a fast worker," he said to his sister. "In fact, you've done such a great job raising grades already that Principal Zeus has decided to end the contest today."

"Which should help ease tensions around here. No more fighting," said Aphrodite.

"Today?" Eris echoed. "What? As in *now*?" She looked at Aphrodite and Athena for confirmation. When both girls nodded, she appeared to shrink a couple of inches before their very eyes. Eris stared at Ares in confusion. "But I just saw Principal Zeus before breakfast and he said—"

"My dad has been known to change his mind," Athena interrupted her to say. "You just learn to go with the flow."

"Yeah. One of the perks of being King of the Gods and Ruler of the Heavens," added Heracles.

"I see," Eris said. "But what about this?" With a sly glance at Athena and Aphrodite, she reached into her bag and withdrew the golden trophy, setting it in the palm of her hand.

Immediately, Aphrodite's fingers itched to touch the prize. Thoughts of their pinky swearing in the cafeteria earlier and of BFFs seemed to fade away for a moment. What was happening?

She sneaked a peek at Athena and saw that she was

gazing longingly at the trophy too, while at the same time clenching and unclenching her fists. No one else seemed bothered. Not even Persephone, who continued to snuggle Adonis in her arms. But then she had never actually *touched* the trophy.

"So if the grades competition is over, since my team was ahead, doesn't that mean I won the trophy?" Athena asked breathlessly.

Aphrodite frowned. "Not so fast. Makhai and Kydoimos cheated on that Science-ology quiz. Don't you think we should at least throw out their scores before—" Her words ground to a halt as Ares chose just that moment to grasp her hand. She looked up at him. Immediately, she understood he was trying to warn her that the trophy was affecting her emotions again. And she clammed up.

Heracles had done the same with Athena, and Athena had clammed up too.

Unfazed, Eris simply sat on the bench again. Setting the trophy in her lap, she pulled some crumpled sheets of papyrus from her bag. "Let me just consult my point tallies," she said, grinning up at Athena and Aphrodite. "Want to hold my trophy while I do?"

Without thinking, both girls reached out. "Don't," Persephone cautioned them in a whisper. "She's only been trying to keep you trophy-tized."

Suddenly, a stiff breeze blew into the grove. *Whoosh!* Eris's score sheets went flying. "No!" she shouted. Adonis leaped from Persephone's grasp to land on the bench right next to Eris, surprising them both.

"Why, hi there, little guy," Eris cooed to him, forgetting the papers and the trophy for the moment as everyone around her scrambled in vain to catch them. As soon as Adonis realized it was her, he panicked, bristling and hissing. *Ssss!*

Leaping off the bench, he raced away. Unfortunately, Artemis had chosen just that moment to enter the grove with her three dogs.

Though the dogs were used to Adonis by now and normally left him alone, the kitten's agitation stirred something inside them. They took off after him. And before Artemis could stop them, they'd chased Adonis up an olive tree!

"Sit. Stay!" Artemis ordered sternly, after she finally managed to corner her dogs. "You guys should be ashamed of yourselves!" she scolded them. Her dogs hung their heads a little and licked her as if to say they were sorry.

Meanwhile, Aphrodite and Persephone tried to coax Adonis down. Only the kitten wasn't budging. From about two-thirds of the way up the olive tree, he peered down at them through the leaves and branches, mewing pathetically.

As soon as the kitten had gotten stuck, Athena had run off to look for Pheme or Eros or some other winged student who could fly to the top of the tree to rescue the kitten. However, she returned minutes later without success. "I brought winged sandals, though," she announced when she returned.

"Adonis loves those," said Aphrodite, shaking her head.

"Oh, good," said Athena.

"No, I mean he thinks they're birds. If anybody goes up there wearing them, he'll leap from the tree to grab them and probably fall."

Athena groaned. "Anybody got another idea?"

"That tree must be thirty or forty feet tall. And up near the top, it's not strong enough for one of us to climb," said Ares.

Persephone snapped her fingers. "There should be a

ladder near the Academy greenhouse," she told Heracles and Ares.

"We're on it!" Ares yelled. He and Heracles took off in the direction of the greenhouse, which wasn't far from the grove. Artemis went too, to take her dogs back to her room.

Mrrowowow! Adonis had begun to yowl piteously. Eris came to stand under the tree, leaving her belongings on the bench. She had shrunk more, Aphrodite noticed. The chiton she was wearing was loose on her now, and its hem hung almost to her ankles. But why?

Eris gazed wistfully at Adonis high above them. In a small, sad voice she said, "He will do anything to get away from me, won't he? I scare him." She twisted her hands together as she peered up into the tree. "It's all my fault he's up there."

"No, it's not," Persephone told her kindly. "Don't forget. Artemis's dogs chased him."

"Pets act like animals sometimes," Athena added. "Which they are, of course. Nothing we can do about it."

"I wonder what's taking the boys so long with that ladder," Aphrodite said anxiously when they didn't return right away.

Mrrowowow!

"Oh, this is awful! Maybe we'll have to try the winged sandals after all," said Athena. "And just take a chance that Adonis won't think they're birds and leap after them."

Aphrodite nodded. "Either that or we'll have to wait here all night, or longer, for him to come down."

Eris cocked her head. Suddenly, she snapped her fingers. "I know how to get Adonis down." Before Aphrodite, Athena, or Persephone could stop her, she swung herself into the tree.

"Be careful," Aphrodite called as Eris scrambled upward, quick as a monkey.

"Don't worry," Eris yelled down to her. "I've been climbing trees all my life. Mainly apple trees, though. Just ask Ares." Then, for some reason, she laughed.

Aphrodite shrugged. She suspected there were lots of things Ares hadn't yet told her about Eris. And most of them probably involved her picking on him, poor guy!

"She won't be able to get Adonis down," Persephone whispered to Aphrodite and Athena. "He won't go near her. In fact, he'll probably just climb higher when he sees her coming after him."

But Eris must have realized that too, because as the nimble girl climbed, she stayed far away from Adonis, keeping out of his sight until she suddenly appeared on a branch a few feet above the kitten's head. Then, reaching down toward him, she called out, "Here, kitty, kitty!"

Of course, Adonis didn't come. Instead, he reluctantly moved downward, one branch at a time, just so he could keep away from her. Which must have been Eris's plan from the start! Staying a branch or two above the kitten, she herded him ever lower in the tree until Persephone and Aphrodite were able to reach up to the bottom branches and safely lift him down.

Eris leaped from the tree just as the boys, accompanied by Hades and Apollo, finally returned with a ladder. Artemis was right behind them. She had brought a blanket they could hold under the tree to catch Adonis in case he fell. Luckily, it wouldn't be needed now.

"Three cheers for Eris!" Aphrodite exclaimed to them. "While you were all gone, she climbed up the tree and rescued Adonis."

All the girls gave Eris a group hug, calling her a hero. Persephone had been cuddling the kitten and cooing to him, but even she joined in with one arm. And this time Adonis didn't even hiss around Eris.

"It was nothing," Eris insisted, all smiles now. Adonis's reaction seemed to surprise and please her.

Just then Persephone spotted her mom's chariot overhead. Taking Adonis with her, she headed off with Hades and Apollo to meet her. Once they'd gone, and only Athena, Aphrodite, Artemis, Ares, Heracles, and Eris were left behind together, Eris's demeanor shifted. In a businesslike tone, she picked up her trophy and said, "About that contest. My figures were on those papers that blew away. Without a recount, I don't think I can declare a winner. So I wonder if Principal Zeus might change his mind again and continue the con—"

"It should be mine!" Aphrodite blurted. Then she put a hand to her lips, startled to hear herself say the words. Part of her wanted to call them back, but another part— the part that was under the trophy's enchantment— let the words stand and caused her to speak on. "The inscription on the trophy's base says *For the Fairest*," she quickly told everyone, in case they'd never noticed.

"So?" Athena said, her tone going icy as talk of the trophy raised her competitive instincts too.

Aphrodite fluffed her golden hair with one perfectly manicured pink-fingernail-polished hand. *Did she have to spell it out?* "Well, I *am* the goddessgirl of love and beauty."

"So?" Athena said again. "*For the Fairest* could as easily mean the trophy is meant for the one who is the most *fair* and *just*. As in *justice*. As in the goddessgirl of wisdom. And that would be *me*."

The two girls glared at each other as Eris held the trophy between them. From the corner of her eye, Aphrodite glimpsed Ares and Heracles exchanging looks of concern. But she couldn't seem to break free of the trophy's enchantment, and neither could Athena.

"I'm sorry," she told Ares helplessly. It took some effort to send Athena an apologetic look, but when she did, Athena returned it.

"Me too," Athena replied, "but I can't help it. I want that trophy too."

"Well, if the contest continues, one of you will win it in the end," Eris coaxed. She'd begun to grow taller again. More powerful.

"Wait!" Ares said, sounding desperate. "Maybe we could flip a coin to decide the winner."

"Huh?" said Heracles. "That would end the contest, all right. And maybe stop team members from fighting. But what about the enchant—*oof!*" Ares had elbowed him in the ribs.

"God-dude! What'd you do that for?" Heracles complained, rubbing his side. Aphrodite was wondering the same thing.

Eris scowled at the two boys. Did Ares fear his sister would grow angrier still if she guessed they all knew for sure that the trophy was enchanted? Aphrodite wondered even in the midst of her longing for it.

Ignoring the boys now, Eris held the trophy even closer to her and Athena. "Touch it," she said to them, her eyes glittering. "You know you want to."

With a huge effort of will, Aphrodite took a deliberate step backward. At the same time, Athena did too. The two girls locked eyes, and as they did so, Aphrodite felt a mutual softening in their gaze. *Athena is my friend,* said a small voice inside her head. *Friendship is more important than any old contest or trophy.*

Athena smiled at her, and she smiled back. Was it possible they were having similar thoughts? As if sensing that help was needed, Artemis joined the two girls, and they all linked arms. Perhaps it was that little bit of extra support that enabled her and Athena to break free of the trophy's hold over them. At least for now. Because unlike poor Eris, the goddessgirls' strength came from friendship, *not* discord.

Thinking about that, Aphrodite got the best idea ever. An idea that was sure to satisfy everyone, no matter how the coin toss came out. She glanced over at Ares. "Okay, let's do it," she said.

Eris let out an exasperated sigh, but luckily, she kept her temper.

Ares reached into the pocket of his tunic only to come up empty-handed. "Anyone got a coin?" he asked, looking around sheepishly.

Heracles came up with one and handed it to him. Ares examined it, saying, "Never seen one like this. Where did you get it?"

"It's an old Trojan coin. Cassandra gave a bunch to

Apollo, and he gave one to me." Cassandra was Apollo's crush, and though she and her family lived in an apartment in the Immortal Marketplace now, they were originally from Troy.

"That's her brother, Prince Paris, on the 'head' side," Heracles went on to explain. "The walled city of Troy is on the 'tail' side."

"Okay, then," said Ares. "We'll use it. Heads or tails?" he asked Aphrodite and Athena as he flipped the coin in the air. "Heads!" Aphrodite called out as at the same time that Athena shouted, "Tails!"

Ares caught the coin as it fell and deftly flipped it onto the back of his left hand, keeping the coin covered with his right.

"Ready?" he asked the girls.

"Ready!" the girls called back.

12

Paris Decides

Ares and Aphrodite

ARES UNCOVERED THE COIN. "HEADS!" HE announced. "Looks like Paris has decided the winner. It's Aphrodite." He didn't much like the idea of her taking possession of the enchanted *For the Fairest* trophy, though. Who knew if it might continue to cause trouble? But at least the contest was over.

To his astonishment, Aphrodite didn't immediately

take the trophy for herself. "I need a minute alone with Athena," she said instead.

The two girls stepped to one side of the olive grove to whisper together. Ares and the others watched as Athena nodded her head at whatever Aphrodite was saying to her. What were the they up to? he wondered.

He didn't have to wonder for long. Soon the two goddessgirls returned, standing together. Aphrodite said to Eris, "Athena and I have agreed that the *fairest* decision is for *you* to keep the trophy."

Hearing this, Ares's mouth fell open. So did his sister's. But whereas the girls' decision pleased him, Eris seemed taken aback by it. "But—" she started to protest.

"If there's a real winner in this contest, it's you," Athena told her. "You're the reason MOA's test scores and grades have improved over these last two weeks."

"Yes," Aphrodite agreed. "So, we think that you deserve the trophy much more than either of us do. Besides," she added. "You rescued Adonis!"

Eris seemed to have been caught off guard by this strange turn of events. Ares wondered if anyone else in the group noticed how her height accordioned up and down widly as she tried to decide if she should be pleased that Aphrodite and Athena wanted her to keep the trophy—or annoyed. But in the end, she accepted the trophy back.

"Well, I guess this proves I really *am* the fairest of us all," she said, unable to resist a semi-snarky remark. But then, dipping her head in apology, she added, "No offense."

"None taken," Aphrodite replied graciously.

Athena nodded.

Ares could only stare at his crush in admiration.

Clever, clever Aphrodite! Was it possible they'd all soon be rid of Eris?

Eris slipped the trophy into her bag and everyone started out of the grove. Ares fell into step beside his sister as the others went on ahead of them. Though relieved that neither Athena nor Aphrodite would be taking possession of the trophy, he was worried that it could still cause trouble if it remained at MOA. Somehow, he was going to have to find a way to convince his sister to *leave* the Academy. But before he could bring up that touchy subject, she spoke first.

"You know," Eris told him. "You were right all along about there being an enchantment on my trophy. The Be a Hero shop owner, Mr. Dolos, promised it would affect anyone who touched it, but he—"

"—was wrong about that," Ares said, finishing her sentence. "'Cause it didn't affect *me*." Whether that was because he was her brother or because he was male was hard to say, since no other boys but him had handled the trophy.

Eris shrugged. "Yeah."

They crossed the courtyard, and at the bottom of the granite steps, they caught up to the others. Then, to Ares' utter astonishment, Eris made an announcement. "Hey, everyone. I hope you all won't be too disappointed, but I've made up my mind to return home."

"Really?" said Ares, his heart lifting. This was an incredible stroke of luck! He sensed the collective sigh of relief that swirled around the group, but luckily, Eris didn't seem to notice it.

His sister shot him a wry smile. "Really. I mean, I like it here at MOA, but I miss my friends back at Corinthian Middle School more than I thought I would. "Well, *one* friend, anyway," she said with a blush.

Ares totally missed the blush. He was focused only on the fact that she was leaving. And that she'd made the decision all on her own! In his joy, he surprised both himself and Eris, and probably his friends as well, by giving her a big old bear hug.

"Aha! I knew it," Aphrodite exclaimed in delight to Eris after the hug ended. "That blue letterscroll. You've got a crush!"

"Maybe," Eris said with a hint of her old defensiveness. Then she growled, "But don't even try to weasel his name out of me because I'm not telling!"

"I wouldn't dream of it," Aphrodite said quickly. She wasn't Pheme, after all! She glanced around as they all started up the steps to the Academy. They were way late for second period by now. There were no other students around. But that was okay. She was sure she could sweet-talk Ms. Hydra into giving them all late passes.

"The thing is," Eris confided, "my *friend* wrote me that the principal at Corinthian has agreed to my return." She paused, then added, "You see, I've been zipping back and forth to help out at my old school while you've all been in classes these past two weeks, trying to make amends for that unfortunate roof incident. The roof is fixed now, by the way. School starts up on Monday."

Huh? So she fibbed to Zeus and all of us about being on semester break? Typical, thought Aphrodite. Only it sounded like her school *had* probably been closed for repairs this whole time. Whatever. At any rate, she had to smile a little at Eris's second use of the word "incident."

"When will you be leaving?" Artemis asked the girl.

"Right away, actually, now that I've decided," Eris told everyone. "Since the competition's not going to continue and all. There's nothing to pack since I didn't bring anything from home except my trophy." She glanced at

Aphrodite. "Only I guess I need to return your chiton."

Aphrodite liked that chiton Eris was wearing but it was kind of torn and ruined by now. Besides, she had tons of others she liked as well. "Please keep it," Aphrodite told her. "As a going-away gift."

"Thank you," said Eris, seeming genuinely touched.

Meanwhile Ares had asked Athena for the winged sandals she was holding—the ones she'd hoped to use to help get Adonis down from the tree—and Athena had handed them over. "Take these winged sandals to make the trip back to Earth a little faster," he offered, handing them to his sister. "Next time I'm home to visit, I can get them and bring them to MOA."

"But of course you're welcome here anytime," Aphrodite assured Eris as she sat on a step to put on the sandals. She didn't want the girl to feel hurt. Ares's comment had made it seem like he didn't expect her to ever be back! Eris was his sister, after all, and she did have a sweet side—sort of.

"You know, Zeus was close to offering me a place here at MOA," Eris remarked. "I hope he won't be too disappointed I've decided not to stay." She hesitated before putting on the second sandal, as if reconsidering her decision to go.

"Oh, I'm sure he'll understand," Ares rushed to say.

"Yes!" Heracles nodded. "He will."

"I know Dad appreciates everything you've done," Athena added.

"You've certainly made these last two weeks interesting," added Artemis.

Aphrodite hid a smile. It was clear that they—and probably all of the students at MOA—were anxious for Eris to leave so that things could get back to normal again.

Moments later they all got their wish. With a wave,

Eris left for Earth, clutching her bag with the enchanted trophy and her letterscroll inside. Aphrodite and all the others watched as she skimmed away from the school in the borrowed pair of winged sandals.

"Well, that's that," Athena said with a sigh of relief. "I'll go post a sign declaring that the contest is over."

"Say it was a tie," Aphrodite advised.

"Good idea," said Heracles. "Then maybe everyone can get back to being friends again!"

"What about the prizes Principal Zeus promised the winning team?" Artemis thought to ask.

Ares grinned. "When we tell him my sister has left, I bet he'll be as relieved as we are. He'll probably give the whole student body prizes galore!"

"Now that Eris is gone, taking her discord with her, the idea of making the opposing team be our servants for a day probably won't seem like such a big thrill," said Athena.

"I'd be happy with a week of homework-free days," Aphrodite put in.

"Me too," said Artemis.

"Yeah, I think I've studied harder in the last two weeks than in all my years here put together!" said Ares.

"I hear you, buddy," said Heracles, clapping a hand on his shoulder. "Our brains need a rest!"

As everyone started toward Zeus's office to report on Eris's departure and to get late passes from Ms. Hydra, Aphrodite fell into step beside Ares. She tugged on his arm gently to get him to slow down, and the two of them dropped back behind the others. "You know, I never did get Eris to tell me anything about you when you were a little boy."

"Good," said Ares. Then, when she made a pretend pouty face, he took a deep breath. "Okay, I know I never told you this, but she used to beat up on me when we were growing up. Pinching, taunting, kicking, trying to get me in trouble all the time. I was terrified of her," Then he added softly, "At times I still am."

"Anyone would be. Even Zeus, I bet," Aphrodite said. "Eris can be pretty intimidating when she wants to be!" His vulnerability had touched her. He didn't often show that side of himself.

"Believe it or not, though, I think I'll miss her a little," Ares said. "But not all the turmoil she causes." As they headed off to class, he smiled at Aphrodite. "Want to go to the Supernatural Market for shakes after school?"

"Hmm," said Aphrodite. "That *does* sound good, but I really should study a bit more for my Hero-ology test tomorrow morning."

"Aw, come on. The contest is over," he said. "And it's only one itsy-bitsy quiz. . . ." As she hesitated, Ares pulled something from his pocket. It was the Trojan coin. "I forgot to give this back to Heracles after the coin toss."

She took it form him, sending him a mischievous look. "Want to let Paris decide about the shakes?"

Ares grinned, nodding. "Okay. Heads we get shakes after class? Tails we study?"

Aphrodite flipped the coin high in the air and Ares caught it. And for the second time that day, it came up heads.

"Shakes it is," Aphrodite said, beaming. "Which is fine, actually. I can wait to study till after dinner."

"Yes!" crowed Ares.

Aphrodite smiled at him. Principal Zeus might be a bit disappointed if test scores dipped some with Eris's departure and the grades contest's end. But she figured that by now even Zeus would agree that too much competition was not necessarily a good thing.

Slipping her hand in Ares's, Aphrodite hurried up the stairs with her crush and then off to class.

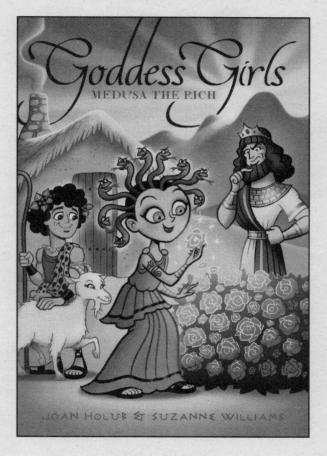

For Activities, Stickers, and More, Join The Academy At GoddessGirlsBooks.com!